Tested by Magic

A Baine Chronicles Novella

Jasmine Walt

Cover art by Alexis Frost

Cover typography by Rebecca Frank

Edited by Mary Burnett

Formatted by Polgarus Studio

If you want to be notified when Jasmine's next novel is released and get access to exclusive contests, giveaways, and freebies, sign up for her mailing list at http://jasminewalt.com/newsletter-signup/
Your email address will never be shared and you can unsubscribe at any time.

Contents

Author's Note

Dear Reader,

Tested by Magic is a companion novella to the Baine Chronicles, my *New York Times* bestselling urban fantasy series. You do not need to read the Baine Chronicles to enjoy this book—however, I thought it might help readers who are new to my work to have a glossary of terms. To that end, I've included a spoiler-free one in the back that you can refer to as you read, or read ahead of time if you'd like.

If you've already read the Baine Chronicles series, these terms will be familiar to you, but you may want to refresh yourself anyway just in case. ;)

To the new reader, welcome to this fantastic world of mages, shifters, steambikes, crazy adventures, and just enough romance to keep you wanting more! And to those of you who have read the previous books, welcome back and thank you! Your support allows me to continue doing what I love most—writing.

Best,
Jasmine

Chapter One

The crack of wood against wood broke the stillness of the cold winter morning. Grunting, I gripped my staff harder and tried to push Roanas back. My arms trembled from the effort, and my mentor grinned at me, his fangs stark white against his black skin. Those tawny lion-shifter eyes glowed with an unholy glee right before he twisted with lightning speed, trying to get past my guard so he could knock me off my feet with a sweep to my calves.

"Like hell I'm going to fall for that again!" I jumped up, out of the way, then brought my staff swinging down with me. But Roanas had already moved, and I had to pivot and bring my staff up again to keep him from braining me from behind. The birds watching from their perch on the backyard fence squawked in irritation as our staffs clashed again, and several of them took flight as my mentor and I exchanged a flurry of blows, pushing each other back and forth across the yard. I had no idea why the birds insisted on hanging out here if they disliked the noise so much. We did this every morning, after all.

"Sweating already?" Roanas commented as he parried yet another one of my blows. "It's far too cold for that, Sunaya."

"We've been at this for an hour," I growled, resisting the temptation to swipe at a bead of sweat stinging my eye. As usual, Roanas was barely winded, and the loose Garaian-style shirt and pants he always wore during training were as dry as they had been when we'd started. In contrast, my tank top clung to my sweaty back and ribs, my cheeks were flushed, and my curls were sticking to my temples. "It's not my fault you're a freak of nature."

Roanas laughed, then sidestepped my next blow and went for my ribs. I parried, twisting to meet him, but my foot slipped on a wet patch of grass and I went crashing to the hard-packed ground. My heart leapt into my throat as Roanas's staff came swinging down, but I rolled out of the way just before it struck me, then swept my own staff straight beneath his knees.

"Oof!" Roanas cried as he landed hard on his ass. Grinning, I knocked the staff out of his hands, then pressed the butt of my own weapon against his throat. The two of us froze—Roanas lying in the grass, and me on my knees above him, staff gripped tightly.

"Very good," he said, curling his fingers around my weapon. "Now why don't you help an old man up so we can have some breakfast?"

I snorted at that, but did as he asked. "Old man, my ass," I said as I followed him inside the house. "You're not even a hundred years old yet."

Roanas eyed me over his shoulder, a droll expression in his eyes. "Perhaps, but you're barely eighteen, child. Compared to you, I'm ancient."

I laughed, then went into the kitchen to whip up pancake batter while Roanas used the shower first. This was our morning ritual—we trained in the backyard for an hour, I got breakfast started while he showered, then he finished off the cooking while I got cleaned up and ready for school.

Except today, I wouldn't be going to school. I would be going to *work*. And I could hardly wait.

As soon as Roanas came into the kitchen, freshly washed and clothed, I bounded up the stairs and into the shower. I was usually in and out fast, but, for once, I took my time washing and dressing, because this was a special day.

I grinned like a loon as I fastened my brand-new enforcer bracelet on my wrist. I'd worn it day and night ever since the day I'd passed the tests last week, taking it off only for my training sessions with Roanas. Today was the day I'd finally get to activate it, to join the ranks of the bounty hunters who chased down criminals and kept the fair city of Solantha safe. I'd show them all what I was capable of—that an outcast from the panther-shifter clan could make something of herself. I'd wow them with my strength and skill and dedication, and Captain Galling would be so impressed he'd have no choice but to give me a crew of my own.

"Sunaya!" Roanas called. "Are you going to daydream up there forever, or are you going to come down and eat?"

"Coming!" I replied, my cheeks coloring a little. Roanas knew me too well. But before I hurried down the stairs, I took one last glance in the mirror. My thick black hair gleamed in the morning light, not a curl out of place, and I'd gone an extra step by putting on eyeliner that made my bottle-green eyes pop. The leather pants and jacket I'd picked up at a thrift shop made me look like a badass, and the crescent knives and chakrams strapped to my body would leave no doubt in anyone's mind as to my profession. The utility belt cinched around my waist was stuffed with protection charms, a set of handcuffs, and some beef jerky for the road.

Hell yeah. I was *so* ready for this.

"Well, don't you look like a hotshot?" Roanas said as I swaggered into the kitchen. Platters of eggs, bacon, and pancakes sat on the stove, and Roanas was already sitting at the table, his plate nearly cleaned. He eyed one of the charms swinging from my utility belt and frowned. "When was the last time you had that checked? You might need to replenish it."

"I'll visit Witches' End soon," I promised as I brought my plate of food to the table. I sat down, then hesitated, my fingers drifting to the circular stone amulet in question. "Do you think anyone will question this?"

Roanas shook his head. "Enforcers wear protective amulets and charms all the time. You don't need to tell them the true purpose for that one."

I nodded, then dug into my food with a little less gusto than I normally would have. As far as everyone knew, I was just a jaguar shifter, tossed out of the Baine Clan because my aunt, the Chieftain, hadn't been able to stand the sight of me after my mother died. No one aside from Roanas and a select few members of the Baine Clan knew the truth—that I was actually half-mage.

And if anyone found out, I was dead. Only full-blooded mages, born into a mage family, were allowed to have magic.

They, and the foreign magic users who lived in Witches' End—immigrants who paid a hefty fee for the privilege to live in the Northia Federation and keep their powers.

The reasoning, of course, was that these immigrants were already fully trained in their magic, and could keep a handle on it without losing control. But those of us who were born with magic into a non-mage family could not be trained, as there were no mages who would take responsibility for us. And the Canalo government certainly didn't want to trouble themselves over our welfare any more than they had to. Their solution was to send mages into the public schools to test all the children for magic. Those who tested positive were given two choices—have their magic stripped or lose their lives.

I had no idea what would have happened if the mages had found out about me. All shifters had a little bit of magic in us—it was what allowed us to change forms. If I had tested positive as a magic user, and underwent the magic wipe, I might not have been able to survive it. Or worse, I might have been turned into a human. A shudder wracked me at the thought. Either one would have been a horrible fate.

Thankfully, I'd never had to find out, because I'd passed the tests with flying colors. I shouldn't have been able to do so—I had magical power in spades, if the few outbursts I'd experienced were anything to judge by. Most of the time, though, I couldn't access my magic at all. It only seemed to come out when I lost my temper, or when I thought I was going to die.

Which, unfortunately, happened far more often than I'd like.

Worried now, I rubbed my fingers against the amulet, which Roanas had purchased for me from a charm shop in Witches'

End. This amulet was meant to contain magic, so that when I got riled up, it wouldn't come spilling out. Roanas had gotten it for me when I was thirteen because I had nearly killed another shifter teen with an accidental outburst of my magic during a brawl. He'd used his influence as the Shiftertown Inspector to sweep that incident under the rug. Since then, he had enforced a rigorous training regimen on me. Kan-Zao, the ancient martial art he'd learned during his travels in Garai, was largely about mental and physical control. The lessons had gone a long way in helping me get a handle on my emotions.

Unfortunately, there was only so much training could do. Shifters were passionate by nature, and when we were threatened, it was hard to control our instincts.

A knock pulled me from my thoughts, and I jerked my head toward the door, nostrils flaring. *A human*, I thought, catching the scent. Male, musk, and leather with the faintest trace of stale blood. My pulse sped up a little—it was an enforcer. It had to be. They were the only humans who came calling to this house.

"I'll get it," Roanas said, his chair scraping back. "You finish eating." He patted me on the shoulder as he moved past me, out of the kitchen and into the living room.

I did as I was told, reaching for another piece of bacon. After all, I could hear the conversation just fine from here—there was no need to go to the front door.

"Good morning, Inspector Tillmore," a gruff voice said. "I'm Enforcer Elin Blackhorn."

"I know who you are," Roanas said mildly. "What can I do for you at this early hour?"

"Do you know of any suspicious out-of-towners who may

have taken up residence in Shiftertown recently?" the enforcer asked. "Anyone who's been flashing money around more freely than usual, for example?"

"Not that I know of." I could hear the frown in Roanas's voice. "Why do you ask?"

"Just keep your ears open," the enforcer advised. "Two banks and a large jeweler have been hit recently. We have reason to believe they're all being done by the same gang."

"What makes you think so?"

The enforcer hesitated a moment, as if reluctant to share the information. But Roanas worked with the Guild on a regular basis, and it would be unreasonable for the enforcer to expect Roanas to cooperate without divulging *something*. "In each case, the robbers dug beneath the buildings and directly into the vaults to steal gold and valuables. After the first two hits, other establishments around town started hiring extra security, but the guards at the jewelry shop were knocked out by some kind of sleeping spell. Probably an illegal charm. The Canalo Bankers' Association has set a record-breaking bounty for anyone who catches the gang."

I sat up straight at that, my bacon forgotten. *Record-breaking bounty?* I listened harder, eager to catch any other details I could. What if I could somehow cash in on this? I bet I'd be the first rookie to take down a case that big. I'd set a record of my own!

"Why do you think the robbers are strangers?" Roanas asked.

"There was a similar rash of break-ins in Baro," the enforcer said.

I frowned. Baro was the capital of Inara, one of the Federation's Midwestern states. Canalo was on the West Coast—nearly a thousand miles away.

"Only two months ago, by my records. We're contacting Enforcers' Guilds in other states to see if any other towns have been hit by the same gang. I have a hunch that they might have done a few other break-ins on their way to Solantha. Several crews are on this case, so it's a race to see which one of us catches the bastards first. Any tips would be much appreciated," the enforcer added, a note of urgency in his voice.

I didn't wait to hear any more. Leaving the rest of my breakfast on the table, I bounded out the back door to grab my bicycle. If several crews were on the case, I had a chance to get in on this. And I damn well wasn't going to waste it.

Chapter Two

I whizzed through the city on my rickety bicycle, shooting past the border of Shiftertown into Rowanville. Rowanville was the only place in Solantha where shifters, mages, and humans lived together—mages usually lived in the Mages Quarter, humans lived in Maintown, and shifters lived in Shiftertown. Apart from Solantha Palace in the Mages Quarter, the few government buildings in our town were all located in Rowanville, the Enforcer's Guild included.

As I approached the tall, dingy grey building that served as Solantha's bastion against crime, a steambike whizzed past me, nearly knocking me off my own vehicle. I choked on the cloud of hot steam, then glared at the shiny machine as it sped past me and into the Guild's parking lot. Dammit! Even my strong shifter legs couldn't pump hard enough to keep up with steampower. I'd coveted a steambike since I was barely a teenager, but they were expensive as hell. Many of the enforcers had them, and I tried not to glance at the row of shiny bikes parked outside the Guild as I tucked my rickety little bike into the corner.

You'll get one of your own soon enough, I told myself as I squared my shoulders. *You just need to catch some fat bounties first.* In a city with half a million people, where crime was alive and well, how hard could that be?

Putting my visions of grandeur aside for the moment, I pushed open the door, then swaggered inside as if I owned the place. I'd been in here plenty of times during the past few weeks as a trainee, but I still got a little jolt of excitement as my boots clopped against the scuffed cream tiles. The lobby was buzzing with activity—enforcers coming and going via the bank of elevators along the back wall, and trainees upfront dealing with the rows of people who'd come here to report a crime or check in on a case. I'd been one of those trainees barely a week ago, and I gave them a little salute as I sauntered past. They watched me with a combination of hope and envy, and I knew they were counting down the days until they could get out from under the thumb of the tyrannical desk sergeant and join the ranks upstairs.

Trying not to look *too* eager, I hurried into an elevator with a few other enforcers. They eyed me with looks ranging from curiosity to resentment, and I stared resolutely at the steel door, ignoring them. I knew that the older enforcers didn't always like new blood—after all, enforcers made their living off bounties, and the more enforcers around, the more competition we'd have to contend with. Hopefully, the most successful crews would feel differently, since they were already at the top of the pole. From what I'd observed, there weren't that many shifters in the Main Crew, so maybe I could convince them that I'd be an asset.

The enforcer at my left elbow raised an eyebrow as I stepped off at the third floor, which belonged to the Main Crew. I tossed my curly hair over my left shoulder and marched through the rows of desks, ignoring the way the enforcers sitting at them eyed me with barely concealed disdain. I wasn't going to let these guys intimidate me, not if I wanted to be one of them. Most enforcers were assigned to a crew, and the Main Crew tended to get the most lucrative dockets. Since Captain Galling hadn't assigned me yet, I planned to get the Main Crew to take me in before he stuck me with a lesser one. I'd already thought out my speech to the crew foreman—I wouldn't beg, but I'd propose a probationary period, where they'd give me a month to prove my worth. I'd heard they were two enforcers short after a recent accident, so I should have a chance.

But before I could reach the office of the crew foreman, located toward the back, a huge male stepped in front of me. He was six foot three and around two-hundred-and-fifty pounds, with a thin layer of orange fuzz covering his blocky head, beady blue eyes, and knives strapped all over his body.

"Hey." He jerked his square chin at me. "What's a rookie like you doing here?"

"I'm here to see Foreman Crowley." I met his scathing stare with one of my own, refusing to back down. I'd be out of here in an instant if I showed even an inkling of weakness. "What's it to ya?"

"We don't let riffraff come in here to bother the boss," Carrot Top said, folding his massive arms across his chest. "Tell me what you want, and I'll tell you if you can have it."

I curled my lip at him, refusing to be dissuaded. "I didn't come here to talk to you, Carrot Top. Let me pass." *Stay calm,* I told myself. *Don't let him rile you.*

Another enforcer stepped up to block my path—this one a brunette with a heavily made-up face, high ponytail, and a sword swinging at her leather-clad hip. "Move along, girly. This place isn't for rookies like you. The Main Crew only takes the best."

I raked my gaze over her. "And you're supposed to be part of the best? Don't make me laugh. I could beat you in combat without breaking a sweat." She was just a human, after all—no match for my shifter strength and speed.

I tried to shoulder my way past her, but Carrot Top shoved me back. "You're not getting past us until you tell me what you want," he said. He raised an eyebrow as he noticed my curling fists, then added, "Think twice before you decide to use those. You might be a shifter, but you're outnumbered here."

Dammit! I didn't have to look around to know that every eye in the room was trained on me now. And there were a lot of eyes— from over a dozen people. My magic began to bubble in that secret place in the center of my body, and the amulet hanging from my waist grew warm in response. Fuck. The last thing I needed to do was lose control in a place like this, where every last person would jump at the chance to apprehend me.

By Magorah, Sunaya, a voice whispered in my ear. *You're like a lamb walking into a den of wolves. What were you thinking?*

That I need a fucking job, and I want to stand for justice, I snapped back at it.

"Look," I said to Carrot Top, trying for a placating smile even though my fangs were aching to rip his throat out. "I'm not trying to cause trouble. We're on the same side, right? And you don't seem to have a lot of shifters on your crew." This time, I did glance around—there were only three shifters in the entire room. "You guys could use someone like me. I'm more than ready to prove it."

The brunette laughed incredulously. "Oh, you came to beg the foreman to let you into our crew? Talk about naïve." Her red lips curved into a cruel smile as she stuck out her boot. "Why don't you get down and polish these with your tongue? Maybe if you do that for a month, I'll consider putting in a good word for you." Her scathing tone cut across my already-taut nerves. "Or not. We don't need any more shifters. Why don't I show you the way out?" Her hand drifted toward the knife in her belt.

Before she could pull the weapon out, I punched her in the nose. Bone and cartilage crunched beneath my fist, and she shrieked as blood spurted from her perfect nose. Savage pleasure filled me as she stumbled back, clutching at her face with one hand. I danced out of the way as she hurled a dagger at my shoulder.

"You bitch!" Carrot Top lunged for me, but I was too fast. His momentum sent him careening past me, and I kicked him in the knee to send him down. More enforcers surged out from behind their desks, and I drew my crescent knives, getting ready for a fight. I wasn't going to let these assholes treat me like I was vermin. Not when I was stronger than almost all of them.

"What is the meaning of this!" The door flung open, and Foreman Crowley came storming out. He was an imposing man, an inch shorter than Carrot Top, with close-cropped blond hair and pale brown eyes that burned with outrage. "This is an office space, not a fighting ring!"

"She started it," the brunette howled, jabbing a bloodied finger at me. She had a handkerchief clutched against her nose.

"This rookie punched me in the face for no reason!"

"That's not true!" I started to argue, but then swallowed my words as Crowley stalked toward me.

"I don't know why you decided to come in here and disrupt my crew," he said in a soft, deadly voice. "And I don't care. No one harms a member of my crew without paying a price." He grabbed me by my upper arm and began dragging me back toward the elevator.

"Where are you taking me?" My bloodlust had faded completely now, fear pounding through my veins instead. By Magorah, was I about to lose my enforcer shield on my very first day over a stupid fight?

"To Captain Galling, so he can decide your punishment."

***

I spent the rest of the morning cleaning the bathrooms on all four floors of the Enforcer's Guild. Captain Galling told me I was lucky that Roanas had such a good relationship with the Guild, or my punishment might have ended up far worse. My cheeks burned with shame as I scrubbed the crusty toilets, and I prayed to Magorah, the shifter god, that Captain Galling hadn't told Roanas about my behavior this morning. I wasn't sure I'd be able to stand going home, knowing that deep look of disappointment would be etched into the lines of his dark face.

By Magorah, but why did I have to lose my temper like that? Yeah, so that brunette had been a total bitch, and she'd deserved that punch in the face. But Roanas had warned me countless times that some of the enforcers were bullies, and that I should ignore any taunts and provocations. By giving in to my emotions, I'd tossed any chance I had of joining the Main Crew straight out the window. Maybe I could still somehow squeeze myself onto one of the other crews, but it wouldn't be any of the ones assigned to the big robbery case. No, those snobby bastards would stay clear of me now that I'd shown them I wouldn't be reduced to a mere lackey.

She wouldn't have let you into the Main Crew even if you had *licked her boots for a month,* I assured myself. A stuck-up bitch like that would have just gloried in her subjugation of me, then kicked me to the curb when she had no use for me anymore.

After I finished scrubbing the toilets, I went back up to the fifth floor and waited in the little reception area outside Captain Galling's office for the next two hours. Lunchtime passed, but I didn't budge despite my growling stomach. He'd told me that he was going to give me a case when I was through with my punishment, and to stay here until he called for me. I wasn't about to piss him off by going to get lunch, even when a delivery boy came in with a box that smelled very much like orange chicken and pork-fried rice. My mouth watered as I watched the receptionist carry it into Captain Galling's office, and it was all I could do to stay rooted to the couch. Several enforcers came and went, and each time one was admitted into the Captain's office, I grew a little angrier. Was he deliberately torturing me?

"Enforcer Baine," the receptionist said, pulling me from my internal grumblings. "The Captain will see you now."

Finally, I thought but didn't say as I rose. I thanked the receptionist, then walked past her desk to the door and opened it. Captain Galling's office was surprisingly utilitarian, with none of the fancy trappings I'd expected from a man of his rank. A large desk and a file cabinet took up half of the space, shelves lined the left wall, and there was a cot in the corner, which I assumed he slept on when he had to work overnight. The only personal touches were a few framed photographs on his desk of his wife and children, and a couple of award certificates on the back wall from the various neighborhood councils in Solantha.

The man himself sat in his chair, his hands folded atop his desk as he regarded me. He was a handsome, stern-faced man in his late forties, with a touch of salt and pepper at his temples, and crow's feet that branched out from the corners of his blue-black eyes. Unlike the rest of the enforcers, he wore a suit, and the slight softness of his body told me that he hadn't donned enforcer leathers in quite some time. I was startled to see an auburn-haired woman, who was maybe twenty-three, rise from one of the visitor's chairs. As she unfolded her lithe body, clad in leather and weapons, I realized she was one of the enforcers who'd passed by me earlier.

"Enforcer Baine, this is Annia Melcott," Captain Galling said. "Enforcer Melcott, meet Sunaya Baine. She's our newest recruit."

"A pleasure," Annia said, holding out a slender hand. Her dark brown eyes twinkled as she measured me. "I've heard interesting things about you."

"I'm sure you have." Refusing to take the bait, I grasped her hand, taking a second to study her. Her palms were calloused, her nails trimmed, but they were painted a deep burgundy with gold designs on the ring fingers. Her leathers were high quality, certainly not bought in a secondhand shop, and her boots looked brand new. The scabbard of the sword leaning against the chair she'd vacated was made of lacquered wood, and the cross-guard of the sword was carved into an intricate pattern. Not a throwaway weapon—it was expensive, and the knives she wore looked to be of similar quality. Her auburn hair was sleek and shiny, her face was flawless, and the confident way she carried herself told me she was used to getting what she wanted.

I hated her on the spot.

"So," Annia said in a voice like silk as we sat down. "Why have you called Enforcer Baine in here? I thought we were discussing a new case for me?"

"The case is for both of you," Captain Galling said, and I stiffened. I was going to have to work with this uptown girl? I had no doubt she came from money—she was probably in this line of work for the thrills, not because she actually needed the cash. "It's up to you two how you're going to split the bounty, which isn't anything to write home about, mind you." He raised his eyebrows at me, as if that last statement was specifically for me.

"I can handle it on my own," I insisted as bitterness welled up inside me. A small bounty meant a small case, and being forced to split it with another enforcer was just an added insult. "I don't need a partner."

"Neither do I," Annia said, her cupid's bow mouth turning down. "You know I work solo, Captain. Why are you having me team up with a rookie?"

"This particular case would be best solved by both a shifter nose and a human," Galling said brusquely. "Since it is impossible to combine those qualities in a single person, I am putting both of you on this case." His eyes narrowed as he looked between the two of us. "If you can't work together, there are other human and shifter enforcers I can give this to." His forbidding tone left no doubt in my mind that if I refused to cooperate, this would be the last case he gave me.

"No!" Annia and I both exclaimed at the same time.

We exchanged looks of annoyance, and then Annia said to the captain, "Of course we'll take the case, sir."

"Excellent." He tossed a manila folder at me, which I reflexively caught. "Now get out of my office, and don't come back until you've solved this."

"Let's go to my desk," Annia muttered as we left the Captain's office. "We can study the file together."

I said nothing, simply clutched the folder a little tighter as Annia and I took the stairs to the fourth floor, one level down. Of all the people Captain Galling had to stick me with, why *her?* It was bad enough I'd have to share this bounty with someone—having to give half of it to a snooty rich girl who didn't even need the money was like rubbing salt in an open wound.

The fourth floor of the Enforcer's Guild was where the smaller crews and solo enforcers worked, with workstations spread out across the open-floor space. Annia's was toward the back—a simple desk with a typewriter, various office knickknacks, and a framed picture of a freckle-faced redhead who couldn't be more than ten. I frowned curiously as I noticed the oil smudge on the girl's cheek, and the aviator's cap and overalls she wore.

"Who's that?" I asked as we sat down. I didn't feel guilty about prying—sticking my nose into other people's business was an acceptable trait for an enforcer.

"Hmm?" Annia glanced toward the photograph, and her dark brown eyes warmed. "That's my kid sister Noria. She's always tinkering with stuff in our late father's garage. I think she's going to be an inventor someday, if Mother doesn't kill her first." She laughed softly.

"Oh. That's nice." I shifted in my chair, a little uncomfortable now. I didn't want to think of Annia as a human being—someone with a family, with a heart. So instead, I opened the file and pulled out the case sheet. "You want me to read this out loud?"

"No!" Annia glanced around, then scowled at me. "We don't want another enforcer overhearing the details. They might decide to snag the bounty for themselves. We'll read this silently, then discuss."

"Right," I muttered, my cheeks warming as we leaned over the paper. Annia shouldn't have had to remind me of that. No wonder the Main Crew had tossed me out on my ass—I was acting just like the rookie they'd accused me of being.

The details of the case were sparse and straightforward. A middle-class Maintown couple, Marlin and Coralia Thotting, had reported their daughter missing. Ten-year-old Cerlina Thotting was an only child who'd gone to school the day before yesterday, but never returned home. Our task was to find the missing child.

"We'll be splitting this fifty-fifty, I'm guessing?" I asked when Annia finally leaned back from the folder.

"Of course," Annia said. "The credit is more important to me than the money, but as long as you pull your weight, I don't see why you can't get equal credit."

"Likewise," I said, even though that wasn't strictly true. I wanted to move out of Roanas's house and get my own steambike, not necessarily in that order. And if I wanted to do that any time soon, I needed to prove myself on this case so Captain Galling would trust me with my own bounties in the future. If that meant working with a human socialite playing enforcer, then that was what I'd do, even if it was a damned bitter pill to swallow.

Chapter Three

"Well?" Annia raised an eyebrow. "Aren't you coming?"

I folded my arms across my chest as I stared at the steambike Annia was sitting astride. It was a beautiful, sleek machine, all chrome and steel, with roses and thorns etched into the gleaming black finish. And it had no doubt cost a fucking fortune.

"We can't all afford steambikes," I muttered, trying to sound like I wasn't absolutely burning up with envy inside. "My bike's over in the corner."

Annia glanced over at the rickety bicycle I'd indicated with a jerk of my chin, then rolled her eyes. "You're not riding that. You'll never be able to keep up, and I don't want to wait around for you. Get on." She scooted forward, then patted the seat behind her. "There's a half-helmet and goggles in the right saddlebag."

I wanted to protest, but I didn't have a leg to stand on. Annia was right—I would take way too long on my bicycle, and if we were running this case as partners, we needed to stick together. So, I grabbed the helmet, then slung a leg over the bike and perched on the seat as far away from Annia as I could manage.

"What—are you afraid I've got fleas?" Annia reached back, and I let out a startled yelp as she grabbed my waist and yanked me against her. "Snuggle up, kitty cat. I don't need you turning into roadkill during your first day on the job." Her silken voice held a distinctly amused note, and my ears burned. Was she teasing me? Before I could ask, she slid her visor down, then started up the engine. I cringed as it emitted a high-pitched whistle, and gripped Annia's waist a little harder than I should have.

"Hey." She flicked her visor up again. "I said snuggle, not suffocate. I have to drive this thing."

"Sorry." I loosened my grip, and she kicked off, shooting down the street.

As we sped through traffic, I tried to forget that I had my arms around a stranger, so I could enjoy the ride. But since I was only wearing a half-helmet, the icy wind ripped at my skin, and I was forced to tuck my face against Annia's shoulder. She smelled like floral soap and spice, mixed with leather and that tang of old blood.

Like the enforcer who'd come to visit this morning, I thought. Annia must have seen combat, and had drawn blood during it. Of course, I'd known she couldn't be just good looks and money—the sword at her side was a real weapon, and the calluses on her palms told me she practiced with it regularly. But it was beginning to sink in that she might actually be able to do a bit more than charm her bounties into submission with those long eyelashes and that silken voice.

Stop thinking about Annia, I told myself sternly. *You're on the job now.* I turned my attention back to the case sheet, which I'd memorized before we left. We were on our way to interview the parents in their Maintown residence, to get what details we could. *Were they good parents?* I wondered, or had they been harsh, as Aunt Mafiela had been to me? I couldn't imagine behaving so cruelly toward my own child, and even my aunt had treated her own children well enough. But parental abuse did happen.

Still, I shouldn't assume anything. I had to approach this case with an open mind. Right now, there were two main possibilities—either the child had run away from home, or she'd been kidnapped. If she was a runaway, we might be able to find her loitering in one of the hidey-holes in the city that homeless children used. They were usually abandoned buildings or hidden alleyways tucked behind industrial complexes. I was intimately acquainted with most of them, as I'd moved between several of those places during the months I'd been a homeless child. I tried not to think about those dark days after Mafiela had kicked me out, before Roanas had found me and taken me in. As a shifter, I'd been able to use my abilities to avoid the pimps who preyed on runaways, but other children hadn't been so lucky. Hopefully, little Cerlina hadn't already ended up in the greedy clutches of men like that.

Annia pulled up in front of a townhouse located at the foot of one of Solantha's many hills. She parked the bike, and we stood outside for a moment, studying the space. It was a two-story home, constructed of dark brown stone, with a small yard in front. The bushes were trimmed, and though the planters beneath the windows were barren, I had a feeling they were full of colorful blossoms in the summer. The curtains in the windows were drawn shut against the afternoon sun, and there was not a spot of grime on the sparkling glass—or on anything else that I could see.

"It's a nice place," Annia said, tucking her hands into her jacket pockets. "Looks clean and well maintained from the outside." She glanced at the steamcar parked in front of the garage, then added, "That model is at least five years old, but the paint looks new. It's been taken care of."

"Yeah. Looks like a good home." But I knew from experience that just because a house looked nice on the outside didn't mean all was well behind closed doors.

Since Maintowners weren't always friendly with shifters, I let Annia take the lead, following her onto the porch and stepping back ever so slightly as she knocked on the green-painted wooden door. I picked up the sound of a chair creaking, then footsteps pattering against a carpet. They drew close, stopping just outside the door, and I caught the scent of a woman, mixed with a subtle fragrance. Probably checking us out through the peephole.

The locks clicked as they disengaged, and the door swung open to reveal a woman with sable hair and milky skin who looked about thirty-five. She wore a high-waisted grey dress that flattered her figure, drawing attention to her large bust and away from her thicker waistline. Her pale skin seemed stretched too tight across her face, and the dark circles beneath her hazel eyes told me she hadn't slept well.

"Good afternoon," she said, her voice slightly hoarse. "You're from the Enforcer's Guild?"

"Yes, ma'am," Annia said gravely. "I'm Enforcer Annia

Melcott, and this is my partner, Enforcer Sunaya Baine. We spoke on the phone a little earlier."

"Yes, we did." The woman's eyes flickered briefly as she glanced toward me, and I knew she wasn't entirely comfortable with my shifter heritage. But she stepped back and waved us through. "Please come in. My husband had to run out to the store, but he'll be back any minute. I told him you were coming."

As I'd anticipated, the interior of the house was as welcoming and clean as the outside. Hardwood floors gleamed beneath our feet, and cream-colored paper with a flower pattern covered the walls around us. Directly in front of us was a carpeted staircase that led up to the second floor, and to our left was a sitting area with green corduroy couches and small, dark wooden tables. A fire danced merrily in the stone grate, at odds with the anxiety and grief etched into Coralia Thotting's face.

Mrs. Thotting offered us tea and cookies, and I did my best not to scarf them all down as we talked. That was incredibly difficult, as I hadn't finished my breakfast and had skipped lunch. The aching hunger in my stomach, which had faded into the background, came roaring back as soon as those cookies, smelling so wonderfully of sugar and butter, were set down in front of us. Shifters had very fast metabolisms, and we had to eat constantly to replenish our energy.

"What do you and your husband do for a living, Mrs. Thotting?" Annia asked as I munched on a ginger cookie.

"Marlin is an accountant," she said, folding her hands around her cup of tea. She did not bring the liquid to her lips, and I suspected she was using the cup more for warmth than anything else. "He provides well for us, but I also work at a nearby plant nursery for half the day, while Cerlina is in school." Her lower lip wobbled a little.

"I see. So, you're at home to see your daughter off to school, and then home again to receive her?" Annia asked.

"Yes. And she always comes straight here, unless she is going to a friend's house, and she never does that without prearranging it with me first." Tears gleamed in Mrs. Thotting's eyes. "I don't understand why this is happening."

The front door swung open, and a tall man in a dark brown coat and matching hat stepped inside. He shut the door against the nippy air, and Mrs. Thotting stood and hurried over to him.

"You're just in time," she said as she took his hat and coat. Beneath it, he wore a white linen shirt and tan slacks. A lean man, but not slight by any means, with regular features. "The enforcers are here."

"Yes, I see that." Mr. Thotting kissed his wife's cheek, then took her hand and led her back to the couch. His eyes, a steady grey, assessed us as we stood to greet him. "Thank you for coming so quickly."

"Of course." Annia introduced us, then said, "We want to get Cerlina home safe as soon as we can."

"Good," Mr. Thotting said with feeling as he joined his wife on the couch. His big hand wrapped around her small one, and she squeezed his fingers tight enough to make her knuckles whiten. "You should go and question her school then. I tried to make inquiries there, but they wouldn't tell me much. They have to protect the privacy of the other students, or so they claim." His expression darkened with frustration.

"Do you think some of the other children know what

happened, then?" I asked. "Or that a parent could have been responsible?"

Mr. Thotting ran a hand through his dirty-blond hair. "I don't know what to think," he admitted, a note of despair creeping into his voice. "Cerlina goes to a good school. We moved into this section of Maintown a year and a half ago for my work, and she's acclimated very nicely to the new environment. We live in a safe neighborhood. My wife goes to all the parent-teacher meetings, and I attend them when I can. The teachers are wonderful, and the parents we've met seem like good people too."

"Cerlina is such a well-behaved child," Mrs. Thotting added in a soft voice that ached with sadness. "I just can't understand why anyone would do this to her. To *us*." Her voice cracked on the last word.

Annia asked Mrs. Thotting to recount the day that Cerlina went missing, which was two days ago, starting with when she had woken the child up. According to her story, everything was completely normal, and Cerlina had been in good spirits when she'd left for school. There had been no indication that anything unusual was going on in her daughter's life.

"And things are going well here at home?" Annia probed gently.

"Very well," Mr. Thotting confirmed. "Cerlina does her chores, we spend time together as family, and she keeps up with her schoolwork. She would have never run away, if that's what you're insinuating." His grey eyes narrowed.

"We believe you, Mr. Thotting," I said, my tone placating. My sensitive shifter nose told me he was being truthful, and that both parents were genuinely worried about their missing daughter. "But as you know, we have to ask these kinds of questions. We have to be thorough."

"Of course," Mrs. Thotting agreed, her voice a little stronger now. "We want the best for our child. We want her home safe."

"Do you have a photograph of her?" Annia asked.

"I have one here," Mr. Thotting said, pulling out his wallet. He removed a small, rectangular item from it and handed it over—a school portrait. Annia took it from him, and we both leaned in to study the picture. I held in a sigh of relief as I took in the girl's braces and unremarkable features—she might grow into a reasonably attractive woman someday, but as it stood now, she would hardly appeal to the pimps who roamed the streets in search of pretty young girls.

"Has anyone new entered your daughter's life recently?" Annia asked after she'd pocketed the photograph. "Any new friends, or anyone who has visited your family recently?"

"My brother Melan has been staying with us for the last three weeks," Mrs. Thotting admitted. "He's from Nebara. He lost his job there when the company he worked for went under. He's out job hunting right now, or he'd be here speaking with you as well. He's never shown any ill-intent toward Cerlina—the two of them have been getting along very well. I won't entertain the idea that he had anything to do with her disappearance." She lifted her chin, her gaze challenging now.

"May I see your daughter's room?" I asked. "It would help us to get a sense of her as a person." *And we might be able to find some clue about what happened to her,* I didn't add.

"Yes," Mrs. Thotting said, rising. "It's right upstairs."

We followed the parents up to Cerlina's room, which was located just to the left of the landing. Unlike the rest of the house, it was a bit cluttered and messy, with stuffed animals scattered across the bed and the shelves, and a disorganized jumble of papers on her desk. The room smelled of candy and human girl, and I quickly sniffed out the stash of chocolate she kept under her bed. The shelf next to her desk was full to bursting with adventure novels, and amongst the jumbled papers were drawings of fantastical creatures. Undoubtedly, she had a very active imagination.

"Baine," Annia called over by the dresser. "I found something."

I turned to see Annia pull a glass flask from one of Cerlina's drawers. Frowning, I went over to Annia so I could get a better look. "That looks like the kind of flask the vendors at Witches' End use for their potions," I said.

"Potions?" Mr. Thotting said sharply. "I don't see why my daughter would be buying potions. She doesn't suffer from any ailments." He turned to his wife. "Did you buy this for her?"

"No." The woman's eyes were wide as she watched me take the flask from Annia. "It's empty. Was there anything in it?"

I uncorked the glass, then took a whiff. "Yeah, there was something in here." My nose wrinkled as I tried to identify the scent, a strange mixture of sweet and bitter. "I don't know what the potion was, but I could identify it if I came across it again." I glanced toward Mr. Thotting. "Do you mind if I take this?"

"Please," he said. "Take anything you need."

We left with the photograph and the flask, promising the Thottings that we would be in touch.

As we sped away on Annia's steambike, I couldn't help but wonder why a girl with such a loving and comfortable family would consider running away. Magorah knew I would have given anything to have a family like that when I was a cub. But then again, a runaway case would be so much better than a kidnapping and any of the nightmarish consequences involved in child abduction. I could only hope Cerlina was safely hidden away at a friend's house, and that she would stay safely hidden from the merciless predators of the street until we found her.

Chapter Four

"By the Ur-God," Annia exclaimed. "You eat as much as one of my uncle's horses!"

I grinned at Annia over my burger. "I wonder if I could out-eat a horse," I said, then glanced down at her already-empty plate. "*You* couldn't, that's for damn sure."

Annia huffed, leaning back against the booth. I'd insisted we stop at a diner for food before I toppled over from exhaustion. "If I ate even half as much as you did, I'd be bigger than a rhino." She eyed me enviously. "I'd be eating cheesecake by the pound if I could keep my figure."

I snickered, then glanced toward the passing waiter. "Maybe I'll order some," I said, then took another bite out of my burger.

"You've already ordered three burgers, two servings of fries, and a milkshake." Annia groaned. "Do you really need to torture me by adding cheesecake to the list?"

I waggled my eyebrows at her. "I'll share."

We laughed, and the sound gave me pause. We were getting along. Me, the outcast shifter, enjoying a meal with the rich human girl. Could this day get any weirder?

Annia glanced at her wristwatch. "It's getting close to end of day for Cerlina's school," she said. "We should head over there soon, if we want to interview her teachers and classmates."

I nodded. "Right. No time for cheesecake." I glanced out the window, watching humans hurry along the sidewalks as they walked past the rows of shops and businesses lining the street. It was a little strange to be eating in a Maintown diner. Maintowners occasionally hired shifters when they needed superhuman strength or senses, and Shiftertowners sometimes hired humans for jobs like bookkeeping or tax advice. But aside from work-related reasons, we didn't often venture into each other's territory. Case in point—I was the only shifter in the spacious diner, and it was a happening place. I'd gotten more than a few askance looks from patrons as they'd passed our booth.

"We're also going to need to interview the uncle," I reminded Annia. "Did we get his last name?"

"Yeah, Melan Drombus," Annia said. "We'll circle back to the house after we do the school interviews." She picked up her cup of coffee, studying me over the rim as she took a sip. "Captain Galling was right. Your shifter nose does come in handy."

"Of course it does." I smirked. "I can sense all kinds of things that you can't."

Annia arched a brow. "Like what?"

"Well, if I've got someone's scent, I can track them," I said, dipping a potato fry into my tub of ketchup. "I can identify most poisons in food, drink, and even on a dead body if I get a whiff of their blood or saliva. And I can tell if someone's upset, angry, afraid, and if they're lying."

Annia's eyes widened. "Can you really?" She leaned forward a little. "You know for certain that Cerlina's parents were telling the truth, then?"

I nodded. "To the best of their knowledge, yes. And they're truly worried about their daughter."

"That's impressive." The sincere admiration in Annia's voice caught me off guard. "Perhaps we should work together more often. I usually work solo, but we could solve cases a lot faster by working together."

"Maybe," I hedged, not willing to commit so easily. I was warming up to Annia a bit, but that didn't mean I wanted to regularly split bounties with her. And once I got used to running cases, I didn't think I would need her.

"I've heard that you live with Shiftertown Inspector Tillmore," Annia said. "Why don't you live with the Jaguar Clan? You are a jaguar shifter, aren't you? And you carry the Baine name."

"It's complicated," I said, a little more sharply than I intended. "I don't really want to talk about it."

"All right, then." Annia looked slightly disappointed, but, to my relief, she didn't press. I wasn't about to tell her that my aunt had thrown me onto the streets, or that I was a hybrid. She could assume I was a full shifter, like almost everyone did. Even other shifters didn't know I was half-mage—they could scent that I was a half-breed, but they all figured I was half-human, and that my shifter traits were simply more dominant.

"I wonder if the Main Crew has made any progress with that new robbery case?" I asked, changing the subject. "An enforcer came by my house this morning to ask Roanas to keep his eyes open for any strange shifters in town."

"I can't imagine why they'd suspect shifters," Annia remarked. "If I were them, I'd be looking at someone in Witches' End, since they used a sleep spell. Or maybe even a mage."

I blinked. "That would be a ballsy move, accusing a mage of robbery. Especially since they don't care about money." Mages considered themselves above 'petty' concerns like profit, as they could produce their own gold. Said production was restricted to prevent inflation, but even so, they all lived comfortably, unlike us peons. They preferred to focus their efforts on learning and spell craft, not money.

"Still," Annia mused, tracing invisible patterns on the tabletop with her index finger. "A mage might take up robbery just for the sport of it. You know, for adventure."

I snorted at that, thinking of the Chief Mage and his ilk. Lord Vengar was a crotchety old bastard who cared little for the subjects of Canalo, and the Council was worse. Their only saving grace was that their self-absorbed ways meant they left us to our own devices. "I can't see any of those guys pulling the sticks out of their asses long enough to indulge in an adventure. They love their rules and conventions way too much."

Annia chuckled. "I can see now why you punched Ralla in the face," she said, her eyes twinkling. "You've clearly got a low tolerance for bullshit, and no filter to go along with it."

I grinned sheepishly at that. "I'm a shifter. We're pretty straightforward."

"And it's a refreshing change." Annia pulled out her purse, then tossed a few coins on the table. "Now let's go put that shifter nose of yours to use. We've got a little girl to find."

Chapter Five

"Well, that was a bust," Annia remarked as we walked out of Mrs. Weaver's School for Girls. "We didn't learn anything."

"I dunno about that," I said as we headed for Annia's steambike, which we'd left in the school parking lot. Teen girls dressed in school uniforms swarmed around us as we walked, chatting and giggling amongst themselves as they reveled in the freedom of finally being released from class. "Mara gave us some useful information."

We'd interviewed Cerlina's teacher and classmates, including Mara, Cerlina's best friend. The pretty blonde girl hadn't known where Cerlina could be, but hoped we'd find her soon, especially because several important tests were coming up that they were going to study for together.

"She did tell us that Cerlina's been tense and preoccupied all week." Annia sighed. "I just wish that she, or any of the other schoolgirls, had recognized that flask."

I pursed my lips. "We'll have to show it around in Witches' End, I think. I should be able to sniff out which shop produces the potion, if they stock it regularly."

"Should we go now?" Annia checked her watch. "The shops down there usually close around six, so we don't have much time."

I hesitated. "No, we should do that in the morning, when everyone is more likely to be around. For now, though, I think we should go check out some haunts Cerlina might be hiding in."

"Haunts?" Annia frowned. "What do you mean?"

"There are various spots around town where homeless kids like to hide. I know where a few of them are." I kept my tone casual, as if I only knew about them from passing by rather than personal experience.

We got on the bike and headed Downtown, where the unsavory souls of Solantha made their homes. The Black Market ran out of here every evening from eleven to dawn, always at a different location. The cracked, dirty streets were lined with brothels and clubs where all sorts of illegal activities took place. I instructed Annia to leave her bike in a safe parking lot just a few blocks from the border between Downtown and Maintown, and we traveled the rest of the way on foot.

"Man." Annia wrapped her arms around herself as a chill wind whipped through the dingy streets. "I should have thought to grab a warmer jacket."

I glanced sideways at her. "You won't want to be encumbered by a fluffy winter coat down here," I told her as we passed a textile warehouse. The acrid scent of fabric dye stung my nose, and I grimaced. "Not if you plan to make good use of your sword."

The sun was hanging low in the sky now, backlighting the

grimy buildings as it crept ever closer to the horizon. One by one, the gas lamps began to turn on, lighting the cracked sidewalks and illuminating the faces of those walking them. The locals were easily picked out from the ones who were just here for the thrills—the former wore threadbare, faded clothing, while the latter were well-dressed beneath their coats and cloaks. The prostitutes hanging out beneath the brothel awnings were the only spots of color in this seedy part of town—they were all dressed in skimpy outfits that allowed them to bare their wares for anyone who looked like they might have enough money to pay them. A few even reached manicured hands toward me, grazing painted fingernails against my leather-clad arm as they promised me wicked delights.

"That last offer sounded tempting," Annia murmured with a wink, and I choked back a laugh.

"Thanks, but I don't really swing that way." I glanced back at the prostitute, who waved cheerfully at me. She looked like she actually wanted to be here, but then again, it was hard to tell. They painted those seductive smiles on as easily as the rest of their faces.

Ignoring the brothels, clubs, and gambling dens, I led Annia down the street, cutting toward a bridge that arched over a dirty canal. "This was one of the places I was telling you about," I said as we walked along the sidewalk that ran along the top of the embankment. "Some kid with a spark of ingenuity built a shelter beneath the bridge. A group of kids used to stay in it."

"Yuck." Annia wrinkled her nose, and I couldn't blame her—the canal water smelled foul, bringing back unpleasant memories that I deliberately pushed away. We came to a stop at just the right angle to get a good look under the bridge. "I don't see anything," she said after a moment. "A few planks of rotted wood, but no shelter."

I sighed. "It must have been washed away by a flash flood. It was bound to happen at some point." *And it has been six years since I last huddled under this bridge myself,* I added silently. It would have been more surprising if the shelter had managed to survive intact. I just figured there would still be kids using this spot, but apparently not. I couldn't make out any signs of life down there, not even a sewer rat. "Let's go with Plan B then."

We crossed the bridge, then headed for a cluster of warehouses on the other side. I led the way around the back of a tanning factory, and my heart warmed at the sight of the grizzled old guard snoring away in his seat by the back entrance. Sure, he wasn't the most industrious employee, but he'd let me spend many a night in this warehouse, and I'd been grateful for the shelter.

"Damn," I muttered when I tried the rusty doorknob. "It's locked." I took a step back, preparing to use my brute strength to force the door open even though I didn't want to wake the old man or scare the girls inside.

"Hang on there." Annia laid a hand on my shoulder, then reached into an inside pocket of her leather jacket. I blinked when she pulled out a small leather case and selected one of a dozen shiny lock picks inside. She jimmied the tiny metal rods into the lock. In less than a minute, I heard a decisive *click* as the lock disengaged.

"Not bad for a rich girl," I teased as she put the picks away.

Annia stuck her tongue out at me. "I don't have super

strength, or an internal lie detector, so I've gotta get by somehow."

She pushed the door open, and I cringed as it squealed loudly. Small feet scrambled frantically against the cement flooring inside, and my heart jumped in my chest. "Wait!" I called, keeping my voice low. "We're not here to hurt you! We're just looking for a friend."

"That's what they all say," a dark-skinned girl accused, meeting my gaze boldly. She stood behind a small fire that had been set up in the middle of the concrete floor, along with six other girls who gaped fearfully at us. The girl who'd addressed us pulled a knife from her boot and brandished it, and the others assumed threatening poses, though they kept well behind her. "We're not going to let you take us."

"We're not here to take you any place you don't wanna go," Annia said soothingly. She held up both hands, and I followed suit. "We're just looking for a girl whose parents are very worried about her. Do you mind if I show you her picture?"

The dark-haired girl measured us for a long moment, her golden-brown eyes taking in our bracelets. "You're from the Enforcer's Guild." It wasn't a question.

"Yes." I met her hard stare. She couldn't be more than fourteen, but the girl who stared back at me out of that brittle face was far older than her undernourished body. "We're looking for a girl named Cerlina, around ten years old. Have you seen her?"

The girl shook her head. "Don't know anyone by that name." She glanced around at the other girls, who hadn't moved a muscle. "Any of you know her?" The girls all shook their heads, and their leader shrugged. "Nope, no one here."

"Oh, come on." I planted my hands on my hips. "You guys don't always use your real names with each other. I know I didn't when I stayed here."

The girl's eyes widened. "You stayed here?" She looked me up and down again. "You don't look like someone who grew up on the streets."

I shrugged, ignoring Annia's curious stare. "I wasn't out here for that long—maybe six months before I was taken in. But I remember what it was like. The constant gnawing hunger. The feeling that you could never quite get warm enough, or comfortable enough. The twenty-four/seven exhaustion, because you always had to keep an ear open at night in case the pimps came stumbling into your hideout."

The leader's gaze softened a little, and the other girls seemed to relax as well. "Let's see the picture," she said, gesturing impatiently for us to step forward. "We get a few new faces popping in every now and then."

We closed the distance, and Annia silently handed Cerlina's picture over to the girl. As the other girls gathered around to look at the photograph, I took a moment to study them. They ranged between ten and fourteen, dressed in torn jeans, sweaters, and coats that were clean enough, though worse for the wear. They wore their hair in ponytails or messy buns back from their gaunt faces, and though my nose twitched at the greasy smell of unwashed hair, their faces were clean. They probably sponge bathed themselves whenever they could. Scattered on the floor around the fire were thin pallets and threadbare blankets. In the far corner was a cracked sink and a metal toilet that I didn't remember seeing the last time I was here. Guess the place had gotten an upgrade.

"Sorry," the dark-haired girl said, handing the photograph back to Annia. "We haven't seen her around. She might be hiding out in a different part of town, if she hasn't been taken."

My heart sank. "Thanks," Annia said, tucking the photograph away. "We appreciate your help."

"W-what are you going to do if you find her?" one of the girls, a blonde with porcelain skin who looked about twelve, asked in a soft voice. Her lower lip trembled as she gazed up at us with uncertain eyes. "Are you going to punish her for missing school?"

"Of course not." I gave the girl a reassuring smile. "We're just going to return her to her parents. They'll be so happy to see her that I don't think they'll even consider punishing her. They've been worried sick."

The trembling increased. "I want to go back to my parents," she said in a voice thick with tears. Her big blue eyes began to shine. "I haven't seen them in weeks, but I can't leave because the pimps will find me. They already almost caught me once." She buried her face in the dark-haired girl's shoulder and began sobbing.

"Don't cry, Larina," the other girl said, patting her back awkwardly. "It's going to be okay."

"Do you know how to get home?" I asked the blonde girl. She definitely didn't look like the kind of girl who should be on the streets. How long had she been out here?

She stilled for a moment. "I t-think so."

"And you're sure you want to go back?" I asked, wondering what had driven her to leave in the first place. "Will they welcome you?" My aunt certainly wouldn't have if I'd tried to sneak back into her home.

She cried even harder at that. "Yes. It was just a foolish disagreement. My father is strict, but now I see that he was only trying to protect me."

"Good. Then we'll take you there," I declared. My nose told me that she was sincere and truly not afraid of whatever awaited her back home.

The blonde raised her head, and the hope shining in her wet eyes made my throat ache. "Can you really do that? What about the pimps?"

"They won't bother us." Annia patted the hilt of her sword. "Not if they know what's good for them."

The little girl began bouncing up and down on the balls of her feet, then stopped and looked guiltily toward the dark-haired girl. "You don't mind, do you?"

The older girl shook her head. "No. You go on." She cracked a smile. "We'll survive without you."

Annia leaned in close to me as the other girls gathered around Larina to give her goodbye hugs. "This is heartbreaking. Did you really live on the streets for six months?"

I nodded. "It's a tough deal, especially if you're a girl. I like to think my shifter instincts helped keep me out of trouble. Most runaways get kidnapped within a month or two of ending up on the streets. The ones who make it past that point, like this one," I jerked my head toward the dark-haired girl, "are some seriously tough cookies."

Annia and I each took one of Larina's hands, and we kept her close between us as we walked out. The girl only had a blanket over her thin dress to protect her from the chill, and I didn't want her to catch cold. In silence, we herded her across the bridge, then back up the street toward the parking lot where we'd left Annia's bike. The lot was only ten minutes from here. Once we got there, it would be a piece of cake to get the girl home. The address she'd given us was on the north side of Maintown, not very far at all on a steambike.

"Hey!" A fat, balding man wearing dark sunglasses and a fur coat stepped out of an alleyway, directly into our path. Two tattooed thugs in leather jackets followed suit, flanking him. "Just where do you ladies think you're going?" The man looked straight at Larina, an unholy grin spreading across his face. The little girl let out a terrified squeak and ducked behind Annia, clinging to her thighs.

I pulled a chakram from my pouch. "Straight up your ass with this if you don't get the hell out of my way." They didn't budge, and I suppressed a sigh. Did we really have to do this now? "It's cold, and I'm not really in the mood for a fight, so if you move now, we'll leave you in peace."

Two more thugs joined the man, who grinned at us. "I don't think you're in any position to make demands. I'm happy to let you two fine ladies go, but the girl comes with us. My boss, Big Leo, has plans for this one—those golden curls and pretty blue eyes will fetch good coin for years to come. A sound investment, he would say."

Annia and I closed ranks in front of the girl. "You do realize you're talking to enforcers?" Annia asked, brandishing her bracelet. "We could haul your furry ass to jail right now."

The man laughed, the sound full of contempt. "I don't think

43

so. You're outnumbered." He snapped his ring-covered fingers at the thugs. "Go get Big Leo's property."

The thugs lunged for us, four hulking mountains of muscle that no doubt thought they had this in the bag. I flung a chakram at the nearest one, and he went down in a spray of blood, his decapitated head rolling into the street. Larina screamed from behind me as I ducked a blow from another thug, and I twisted around to see that the third had somehow snuck around me. He grabbed the little girl by the collar as she twisted away, and my mouth dropped open in horror as her skimpy dress ripped open to the waist, baring her mercifully flat chest. I tried to lunge for her, but the thug behind me kicked me in the stomach and sent me crashing to the sidewalk. Thankfully, I'd tightened my abdominal muscles against the blow, but it still sent the breath whooshing out of me. Not wanting to waste the momentum, I backflipped myself onto my feet, soaring over Larina and her kidnapper, but before I had a chance to do anything, Annia buried a knife in his throat from ten feet away. The thug released Larina, blood gushing down his chin and chest as he grasped for the knife in his throat. I snatched the half-naked child up as he stumbled to his knees, turning her face into my chest so she wouldn't see him topple to the ground, his final breath leaving him.

The girl had seen enough death tonight.

"P-please," the pimp stammered, backing away as Annia stalked toward him. She'd dispatched the fourth thug already, and he was the only enemy left. This part of Downtown was thicker with shadows than most, and the few passersby hurried on, not bothering to give us more than a second glance. "D-don't kill me. I was just following orders." Eyes trained on Annia, he didn't see the curb behind him, and tripped backward, landing hard on the asphalt.

Annia pressed a booted foot against his throat, and the man began choking. "Tell your boss," she said, her voice like a lover's whisper as she leaned close, "that Annia Melcott sends her regards. And that one day in the near future, she will *personally* toss his ass into the coldest, darkest cell she can find on Prison Isle." Her lips curved into a vicious smile, and I let out a slow breath of admiration. Uptown girl or not, Annia was one scary bitch right now. "You'd be headed there right now if I didn't have more important things to do. Now get lost."

Annia turned back to us, and the pimp scurried off into the night as fast as his fat legs could carry him. "That was pleasant," she muttered as she leaned down to retrieve her knife from the dead thug's neck. She cleaned it on his coat before returning it to her thigh holster, then glanced toward Larina with concern. "Is she all right?"

I smoothed a hand across the trembling girl's hair. "Yeah, but she's gonna need some clothes. We can't have her walking around like this, even if it is only for a few blocks."

After a quick discussion, Annia and I led Larina into the same dark alley those ugly bastards had come from. Huddling behind a dumpster, I stripped off my clothes and gear, then handed most of them to Annia for safekeeping. The little girl stared at me as I gave her my too-big leathers, her wide eyes taking in my shivering body. The sun had fully set now, and it was colder than a mage's heart out here.

"What are you going to do for clothes?" she asked as she put my leather jacket on.

"I've got a spare coat." Winking, I crouched down on all fours, then closed my eyes and reached into that secret place inside me, where my beast always slept with one eye open. She sprang awake eagerly as I called, and white light poured from my skin, engulfing my body as the change started. Bone and muscle stretched, shrank, and rearranged, fur sprouted from my naked skin, and my face elongated into a whiskered snout. Claws scraped at the cement ground beneath me, my tail swished, and when the white light finally faded away, I was a black panther.

Larina gasped, her eyes wide with fear and awe. "I've never seen a shifter shift before," she whispered, clinging to Annia.

"I've only seen it once myself." Annia patted the girl on the back as she studied me with those dark eyes. "I wonder if it stops getting weird after a while?"

I stuck my tongue out at Annia, then padded toward them on silent paws. Larina let out a startled gasp as I moved close, then nudged my snout against her exposed belly. Giggling, she swatted my cold nose away, then finished buttoning up my jacket. It hung nearly to her knees, so she forewent the leather pants and instead stuck her feet in my boots. I huffed out a laugh at how huge they were on her.

"Go on home," Annia said, her eyes sparkling with amusement. "I'll bring your stuff to you as soon as I'm done with our young friend." I nodded, then licked Larina goodbye. The little girl giggled again, then buried her small hands in my fur. Since it wasn't every day that a human got to pet a shifter, I indulged her for a moment, then loped off into the ever-darkening night in search of a fire escape or a rain pipe sturdy enough to hold my weight. Traveling across town in my panther form was best accomplished from roof to roof, as I knew from previous experiences, and there was no time to lose. Rescuing Larina might have been a rewarding side trip, but there was still another little girl out there who needed our help.

Chapter Six

"It sounds like you've had quite the adventure," Roanas remarked as I downed my third bowl of beef stew. He'd already eaten by the time I arrived home, but had put the pot of stew back on the stove the moment I'd rushed into the house. Buck naked, I had sprinted up the stairs to shower and change before coming back down. "Are you done for today, then?"

I shook my head, then swallowed my mouthful of food. "No. Annia should be bringing my stuff by any minute, and then we'll be going out again." I hoped she'd hurry—I felt naked without my weapons, even though I was dressed in jeans and a t-shirt. "We still have to question Cerlina's uncle. With any luck, he should be home now."

"Ah." Roanas toyed with the medallion that rested on his broad chest, the way he always did when he was thinking. It was a golden disk with runes etched along the outer edge, and a fang stamped in the middle—the mark of his authority as the Shiftertown Inspector. Shiftertown, Maintown, and the Mages Quarter tended to police themselves—the Enforcer's Guild only got involved if a case was brought directly to them, or if it was an interspecies crime. I'd tagged along on many of Roanas's cases. Watching him work was what had inspired me to be an enforcer in the first place. As a half-shifter, I would never be respected enough to become Roanas's successor, but the Enforcer's Guild employed humans, shifters, and even the occasional mage.

"Do you think you might be looking too far afield for little Cerlina?" Roanas finally asked. "Perhaps you haven't delved deep enough into her past, and she's hiding in a place that would be obvious if you only knew a bit more about her."

I opened my mouth to say that a ten-year-old could hardly have much of a past, but a knock at the door interrupted me. "I'll get it," I said, catching Annia's scent. "It's my ride."

"Hey," Annia said when I opened the door. "You ready to go?" She handed over my belongings in a neat pile.

"Yeah, just let me get changed." I hesitated, then added, "Why don't you come in out of the cold?" I moved back to let her inside, then shut the door behind her.

"Hello, Inspector Tillmore," Annia said as Roanas stepped into the living room. "It's been a while."

"Indeed it has." Roanas smiled.

I arched a brow as I looked between them. "You two know each other?" I shouldn't be surprised, since Roanas had a long-time relationship with the Guild.

"I've passed Enforcer Melcott in the halls a time or two," Roanas said. "Though that was when you were still a rookie yourself," he added to Annia. "It seems you've grown into your career. Are you specializing in a particular type of case?"

"Not really, though I like jobs that take me out of town, even if it's simply as a guard," she told him. "I worked for a crew for a few weeks in my first year, but I don't fit in very well with them."

I left the two of them to it as I ran upstairs to get changed. My sensitive ears picked up their conversation easily, and I learned that Larina's parents were overjoyed at the safe return of their daughter.

"By the way," Annia said with a wink as I rejoined them. "Good deeds do get rewarded now and then. Larina's parents told me they'd offered up a small bounty for her safe return— probably too modest to interest any of our colleagues," she added dryly. "We can claim it at the Guild tomorrow morning if we fill out the paperwork."

"That's great!" Small bounty or not, it was still the first I'd earned, and my chest swelled with pride. I'd be piling them up soon enough, and then I could afford to buy things like a real adult.

"Unfortunately, we'll also have to do some basic paperwork to account for the four dead bodies we left behind tonight," Annia added, sounding decidedly *not* thrilled about the idea. "It should only take half an hour, since the location and type of victim speak for themselves."

"Guess that comes with the job," I said with a shrug. If paperwork was the price we had to pay for ridding the streets of scum and seeing that girl home safe, so be it.

By the time we arrived back at the Thottings' house, it was nearly eight o'clock. Normally, I would have felt a little guilty calling on someone so late, but considering the circumstances, I didn't think the Thottings would mind. They wanted their daughter returned safe and sound, and I had no doubt they'd cooperate in any way they could.

"Good evening," Annia said when Mrs. Thotting answered the door. "We've come to speak to your brother. Has he come back from job hunting yet?"

"Oh! Yes, of course," Mrs. Thotting said. She ushered us inside and into the living room. "Have you gotten any closer to finding my daughter?"

"We're still chasing down leads," Annia said. "The case is our top priority."

"Good." Mrs. Thotting wrung her hands, her eyes shining with worry as she looked out the window. "I've been watching the street all day, hoping she'll come skipping up the sidewalk, ready to tell me about some grand adventure she's gotten herself into." A tear slipped down her cheek, and she wiped it away hastily. "I'll go get Melan for you."

She fled up the stairs, and I waited until she was out of earshot before letting out a heavy sigh. "Boy, this is tough," I muttered as the mother's dread and anxiety began to well up in my own stomach. "Have you ever taken a missing kid case before?"

Annia shook her head. "No. Just the usual riffraff. Somehow, this is a lot harder. There's a kind of…helplessness, here." She scrubbed a hand across her face, suddenly looking very tired. "As if hope is slipping away with each passing second."

I let out a breath. "We can't think like that," I said quietly. "If we've already given up in our minds, then we'll never find her." Roanas was constantly drilling that idea into me—that thinking positively was the key to success.

Annia nodded, squaring her shoulders. By the time footsteps sounded on the stairs, we were composed and professional again. Melan was a lean, fit man in his early forties, with black hair and a trimmed mustache. He shared his sister's hazel eyes and full mouth, but his nose was longer, and his skin tanned, as if he spent most of his time outside. He wore a button-up shirt, vest, and slacks that looked well made. Definitely not the kind of clothing someone hard on their luck usually wore.

Maybe that's just his job-interview outfit, I thought.

"Good evening, Enforcers," he said, shaking both our hands with a firm grip. He sat down on the couch opposite us, then clasped his hands between his knees and regarded us steadily. His eyes were calm, but the stiffness in his shoulders betrayed his tension. "Coralia said that you wanted to speak to me?"

"Yes," I said. "This is just routine. We're interviewing everyone who's close to Cerlina. Mrs. Thotting said the two of you got along well?"

A smile softened his face. "She's a bit of an awkward child, but absolutely darling," he said, turning toward the fire. The flames danced in his eyes as he stared into the grate. "My sister is often exhausted by the end of the night, so I'd taken to reading with her at bedtime. She's delightful, her head full of tall tales and daring adventures. It makes me wonder if she decided to run off and join a pirate crew, or some other such foolish pursuit." His expression shuttered.

"Did she ever mention doing such a thing?" Annia asked.

He shrugged. "Only in the way that children do when they're getting carried away. I never took her seriously. Despite her fanciful notions, she is a devoted daughter and a very studious girl. She would never cause her parents such pain by running away like this, without so much as a note." His jaw flexed. "Whatever bounty the Guild is offering, I'll double it. Just find my niece quickly, before any real harm befalls her. My sister had a difficult birth with her, and the doctor said she will not be able to survive another. I don't think she would survive losing Cerlina, either."

We thanked him for the offer, then showed ourselves out. "He seems to care very much about Cerlina," Annia said as we walked down the steps of the front porch. "Was he telling the truth?"

"Oh yeah," I said, sticking my hands into my jacket pockets for warmth. "He was even sincere about the offer to double the bounty, though I don't know how he can afford it, since he's out of work."

Annia frowned. "He did seem quite well dressed for someone who has no income. But maybe he's living off savings?"

I shrugged. "We could poke into it a bit more."

Annia considered it a moment, then shook her head. "We'll circle back to that. He's not a suspect, so poking into his private affairs isn't a good use of our time. For now, we need to trace the origins of that flask."

***

The next morning, after training and breakfast with Roanas, I hopped onto my bike and headed up to the Port. Annia had taken me by the Enforcer's Guild last night to retrieve it, and we'd agreed to split up this morning. While she filled out the paperwork for last night's activities, I was going to Witches' End to track down the flask.

As I pedaled up and down Solantha's steep, hilly neighborhoods, dodging steamcars and whizzing by pedestrians on their way to work, I couldn't help but miss Annia's steambike. Man, but it had been nice to zoom around town on that sleek, sexy machine. It would be a long time before I had enough money to buy my own, and I almost wished I'd had her come with me just so I could enjoy another ride.

Stop being such a lazy ass, I chided myself. I was more than strong enough to endure the bike ride. Besides, it was better that I didn't take Annia along for this. I needed to stop by Madam Charming's shop so I could recharge my amulet, and I didn't need Annia asking unwanted questions about it.

My route took me up past the Shiftertown border and into Rowanville, then northwest to where the Port was located. The tightly packed streets began to thin out as I reached the coast of Solantha Bay, giving way to wider streets, fancier shops, and luxurious apartment complexes that charged a fortune for their waterfront views. The salty sea breeze teased my nostrils, winding its chilly fingers through my hair so it could tug my curls out behind me like a streaming banner. But despite the cold breeze, the sun was shining brightly, its rays bouncing off the white stone boathouses that marked each pier.

The line of piers stretched north and south as far as the eye could see, making up what we called the Port. It was the largest harbor in the Northia Federation, and did a brisk business. Many local shops and restaurants lined the nearby streets to cater to tourists and sailors from all around the world.

I parked my bike on the street, securing it to a lamppost with a lock, then headed south toward Pier Eighteen, otherwise known as Witches' End. This was the section of Solantha where foreign magic users set up shop to ply their trade. They made good coin off the shifter and human populations, who came to this part of town to seek charms, amulets, and cures for their ailments rather than go to the exclusive Mages Quarter. It cost a lot less, and the residents of Witches' End were a hell of a lot friendlier than the holier-than-thou attitude one could expect from the average mage.

Despite it only being nine o'clock, Witches' End was bustling with activity. People strolled along the pier, perusing the plentiful offerings. Tourists could get their fortune read, a charm to ward off nightmares, even love potions, if they walked into the right shop. Some of the things sold here were mildly illegal, but most of the merchandise was aboveboard. If someone was looking for darker magic, they had to go down to the Black Market at their own risk.

I hurried down to the end of the pier, where Madame Charming kept her shop, anxious to get this errand over with so I could get back to the case. But, to my shock, her gauzy curtains and hand-painted sign were no longer hanging in the windows. Instead, dried herbs and cream-colored curtains hung behind the glass, and there was a different name frosted on it. *Over the Hedge*, it said in type that was somehow both blocky and elegant. What the hell kind of name was that?

Scowling, I pushed the wooden door open, determined to get to the bottom of this. A small bell tinkled as I did so, and the scent of herbs, wax, and magic flowed over me. The combination soothed my nerves despite myself, and I let out a breath as I looked around. Madame Charming's dark colors and whimsical decorations were gone, replaced by clean, simple furnishings crafted out of natural materials. The curtains framing the windows were plain cotton, the tables and shelves were made of driftwood, and the colorfully dyed rugs were handwoven. The place was buzzing with activity, several customers admiring various vials and pouches full of herbal concoctions, by the smell of them. Was this an apothecary?

"Hello?" A male voice, crisp and throaty with a strange accent, came from behind me. "Can I help you find something today?"

I spun around to see a man standing behind me, a half smile on his face. He was tall, with broad shoulders that tapered into a lean waist, dressed in an earthen-colored robe with a sage-green sash tied at the waist. His ash-blond hair framed a long, square-jawed face that looked about thirty, with handsome features and striking, cornflower-blue eyes. My heart did a little flip in my chest, and I realized that he was quite attractive.

"Um, yeah." Clearing my throat, I shoved my hormones back down the hole from whence they'd risen. My Heat was only two months off, and the closer it got, the friskier they tended to be. "I was looking for Madame Charming."

The man gave me an apologetic smile. "I'm afraid she closed up shop and moved back to the Central Continent a few weeks ago." He held out a hand, and I noticed his fingers were lightly stained with herbs and dirt. "My name is Comenius Genhard, and I'm the new owner. Is there something I can help you with?"

"Sunaya Baine." I shook his hand, and a tingle shot up my arm and straight down my spine. *Get a grip! No, not like that!* I scolded myself as I squeezed his hand even harder. Flustered, I tucked my hand into my jacket pocket before I could make an even bigger ass of myself. "I'm an enforcer."

"Ah." His eyebrows rose. "Is this official business, then?"

"Yes and no." I hesitated, then reached for the amulet hanging from my belt. I untied it, then passed it over to him. "Madame Charming made this for me, for protection. The magic is starting to wear down, and I need it charged."

"I see." A thoughtful look entered Comenius's eyes, and he traced the amulet with his fingertips. "Protection, you say?"

"Yes." I met his gaze evenly, refusing to betray my suddenly racing pulse. Did he suspect?

But Comenius only nodded, then pocketed the amulet. "Give me a few moments. I'll take care of it."

He disappeared into the back, leaving the clerk at the front desk to attend to the customers, and I took the opportunity to study his wares. Amongst the herbal teas, soaps, and bath salts lining the shelves, there were quite a few potions. According to the labels, they were meant to cure various maladies. I took the flask from Cerlina's room out of my inner jacket pocket, then compared it to the different sizes and shapes of bottles in the shop. None of them matched.

"Here you go." I spun around, my heart in my throat, at the sound of Comenius's voice. He was standing behind me, the amulet dangling from his fingers, with a very curious expression in his eyes. "This should last you another three months, at least."

"Thanks." My fingers brushed against his, and that thrilling little tingle shot through me again. "Guess I'll have to come back to see you again." Did I sound a little breathless? By Magorah, I was on the job!

"You're welcome any time." His eyes twinkled, and his scent changed very subtly beneath his natural herbal, musky fragrance, betraying his interest. He glanced at the shelves behind me, then to the flask in my hand. "Were you looking for a particular potion?"

"No." I gave him an apologetic smile. "I'm afraid this is the 'official business' portion of my business."

His eyes glinted. "Do tell."

I held out the flask to him. "I'm tracking down a missing girl, and I found this flask in her room. We're a bit short on leads at the moment, so I was hoping I might be able to identify which shop she'd bought this from, or at least what kind of potion was in it."

"Hmm." He drummed his fingers along the length of the flask. "I do carry this kind of flask, but I'm afraid many shops in the area will as well, so that might not be your best bet." He uncorked the bottle, then gave it a deep sniff. A puzzled frown settled over his handsome features. "Honeybeetle, dewblood, anise, and a hint of caraway. There are a few others, but too faint to identify since there is nothing left in the flask."

I arched a brow. "You can smell all that?" Of course, *I* could— my sensitive nose had picked out seven different scents in that bottle when I'd taken more time to study it, though I didn't know their names. But how could a non-shifter manage that?

"Of course I can." He gave me an amused smile. "I would be a poor excuse for a hedgewitch if I couldn't identify which herbs were used in a potion. Much like a chef can identify ingredients in a dish by tasting it, I can identify the ingredients in a potion by smelling it."

"Huh." I filed that bit of information away for later—this guy might be useful in the future. "What's a hedgewitch, exactly?"

"We deal in earth-based magic," he explained. "All of our potions, spells, charms, and amulets are created by drawing on the earth's power, as well as using the natural materials Mother Nature provides. There are some who think of us as mere healers," he added, his eyes briefly flashing with annoyance. "But we use magic just as much as any other witch."

"I don't doubt that for a moment." The place smelled strongly of it beneath the herbs and dirt. It was that burnt-sugar scent that clung to mages like a disease—that I was so careful to make sure didn't cling to *me*. I brushed my fingers against my recharged amulet, seeking its comfort. It worked wonders to control my magic, though it wouldn't help if my life was in danger.

"So, do you have any idea what kind of potion this was?" I asked.

Comenius handed the flask back to me. "I've come across a similar combination once, for a particular customer of my late master. The man's daughter was an empath, and such a talent tends to take a toll both physically and mentally. He asked for a potion that would suppress her magic, so that she might walk amongst others without being assaulted by their emotions."

"By Magorah!" I nearly dropped the flask. "There are potions that can do such a thing?" Would such a potion be useful for me? Or would it hamper my ability to shift?

"Yes, though I can't speak to the concoction's effectiveness personally," Comenius admitted. "But my master was very talented, and a man of integrity. I don't think he would have mixed a potion that he didn't believe worked." His expression turned grave. "Whoever this missing girl is, it is likely that she too is struggling with magical issues. I hope that you find her before something bad happens…but on the other hand, I know that if you do, she will be left at the mercy of the Mages Guild and the magic wipes." His eyes shuttered, as if a wall had suddenly slammed down between us, and I flinched inwardly. "I'm afraid I must get back to work now, Miss Baine. Why don't you see the cashier and get settled up?"

"Uh, sure." Flustered, I said my goodbyes, then headed for the register. I'd obviously upset him with the thought that I'd be turning over an innocent little girl to the Mages Guild. Hell, I was upset myself. What was I going to do? I couldn't abandon that girl to such a terrible fate…but it also wasn't my place to decide what to do with her. My job was to find her and bring her home.

My troubled thoughts churned in my head as I left the shop. Even the sight of the Firegate Bridge, stretching tall and proud across Solantha Bay, couldn't distract me from the knowledge that I'd just gotten myself into a huge mess. And I had no idea how I was going to solve it.

Chapter Seven

"Are you all right?" Annia asked as I picked at my platter of fish. "You look a little down. Did you strike out at Witches' End?"

I shook my head. "I guess I'm not very hungry." Annia and I had decided to meet at a nearby seafood restaurant, so I'd headed over here after I'd finished up at Witches' End. As usual, I'd ordered a huge meal, but now that it was in front of me, I couldn't bring myself to eat much.

Annia gave me a droll stare. "That's bullshit," she said. "I did a bit of digging into shifters this morning, after I finished up the paperwork. You guys need to eat constantly to maintain your energy. If you're not feeling inspired enough to eat, then something's *really* wrong."

I sighed, twirling my fork in the bed of pasta on my plate. How the hell could I tell Annia what I'd learned? That Cerlina Thotting was a magic user, and almost certainly hiding out for fear of discovery? I couldn't bring myself to turn information over to the Enforcer's Guild. Cerlina was technically young enough to go through the magic wipe, but sometimes the mages who administered them were careless and damaged the victims anyway. I'd warmed up to Annia in the last day, and she'd proved herself competent as an enforcer. But would she put the girl's welfare above her own desire to claim the bounty?

"Sunaya." Annia leaned closer, lowering her voice. "You can trust me. Tell me what's wrong."

I looked into Annia's dark eyes, round with concern. Her scent told me she believed what she was saying. But *could* I actually trust her with this?

You don't have a choice, I told myself. *The two of you are partners on this case.* Besides, Annia had showed plenty of compassion last night when we'd rescued Larina. She clearly had a soft spot for children, just like I did. I had to believe she wouldn't throw Cerlina under the bus just for the bounty, especially since she kept claiming she didn't need the money.

"You have to promise not to go running to the Enforcer's Guild with this." Annia opened her mouth. "Just *promise,*" I snarled.

She held up her hands. "All right, all right. I promise I won't go to the Guild about this." She crossed her arms over her chest. "Now what's this all about?"

I leaned in close, lowering my voice so that none of the humans sitting nearby could hear. "Cerlina Thotting is a magic user."

"What?" Annia sat up straight, her eyes wide. "How do you know this?"

I explained about my meeting with the hedgewitch, and what I'd learned about the potion. "I don't see why she'd have the potion, if she wasn't a magic user."

"Could be she'd just found the flask somewhere," Annia said, though she didn't sound very convinced. "Or that it belonged to a friend."

I shook my head at that. "I don't think so. And there are always rumors swirling around regarding the next tests—they're done at random, after all." I scowled at that. I knew the Mages Guild did things that way because they liked to keep us peons on our toes. Thankfully, there were whispers that Lord Vengar would be retiring soon, and we would have a new Chief Mage. I could only hope that whoever took the office next would be more humane, and he'd actually give a shit about his subjects outside the Mages Quarter.

"So why didn't you want to tell me about this?" Annia asked. "This information is crucial to solving the case."

"Because I don't want to throw Cerlina to the wolves." I pressed my lips together. "If we report the truth about why she ran away, Captain Galling will hand her over to the Mages Guild to be wiped—executed if the parents refuse the wiping." Pain sliced deep into my chest at the thought of that poor little girl going through such a thing. "I don't care how much gold they're offering—I won't let that happen to her."

Annia regarded me curiously. "I'd say that was treasonous talk, but as a shifter, I figure you don't care." She held up a hand, cutting off my protest. "Don't worry—I won't give up Cerlina to the Mages Guild, and we'll keep the case report short and vague. But we do have to find her. Her parents are worried sick, and who knows what kind of trouble the girl might be in. I've heard that the more agitated a child is, the more prone they are to having magical accidents."

Don't I know it, I silently agreed. Aloud, I said, "Didn't Mr. Thotting mention that Cerlina had moved to her current school a year and a half ago?"

Annia paused, a forkful of food halfway to her lips. "Yes. What about it?"

"Well, we asked all the girls at her school if they knew where she was, and none of them did. But what if she's been in touch with her old friends?" A burst of excitement rushed through my veins. "Do we have the name of her old school? Maybe we can go over there right now."

"You're a genius, Naya," Annia declared. "We'll finish up here, then go back to the Guild so we can call Mrs. Thotting and get the info."

"Excellent." I picked up my fork, then paused. "Naya?"

Annia grinned. "Cute nickname, isn't it? Now hurry up and finish eating."

I shoveled down the food, then reached for my purse to pay for my share. To my consternation, I was short on the bill. "Don't worry about it," Annia said, tossing some coins on the able. "You can pay me back when we get our bounty."

I sighed. "I'm going to need a lot of extra bounties if we keep eating out like this," I complained as we left the restaurant.

Annia clapped me on the back. "You know how you can earn extra money? Keep an eye out for any gold that smells like geranium oil. I overheard some guys from the main crew saying that the last batch of stolen gold had been sprayed with the stuff, so the shifters are gonna try to trace it. If you find any and use it to apprehend the robber, you might just be able to cash in big."

"I sure hope so," I said fervently, but I wasn't about to hold my breath. Let the Main Crew worry about their fancy case. I had a scared little girl to find, and that was more important than a bag of gold.

Chapter Eight

"Looks like your hunch is paying off, Naya," Annia said as she hung up the phone. "You ready to go and follow up this new lead?"

"Hell yeah." After lunch, Annia and I had gone back to the Guild and used her desk phone to call Mrs. Thotting. The quick call had revealed that Cerlina had another best friend, Galia Brennan, with whom she was still quite close, even after almost two years at her new school. Mrs. Thotting had called Galia's mother right after Cerlina went missing, and was told they had not seen her. But little girls could be very good at keeping secrets, and maybe Cerlina had found a way to hide out there without alerting Galia's parents.

We got the address for the Brennans' home, then hopped on Annia's steambike and headed over there. It turned out to be a two-story semi-detached house in one of Rowanville's nicer areas, with a fence that stretched around to what looked like a large backyard, although we couldn't see much of it from the front.

"Doesn't seem like anyone's home," Annia remarked after we'd rang the doorbell a few times. "You hear or smell anyone inside?"

I shook my head. "If there's anyone in there, they're being *very* quiet." But I could scent magic coming from somewhere, very faintly. Could it be Cerlina, or was there some magic user nearby? I glanced toward the fence. "Why don't we have a look out back? Maybe Cerlina's hiding out in the garden shed or something."

After making sure that no prying eyes were watching, Annia and I climbed over the fence and into the backyard. What we were doing wasn't strictly legal, but I didn't think the owners would mind if they knew why we were here. From what Mrs. Thotting had told us about the Brennans, the two families were well acquainted and on good terms.

"Well, would you look at that?" Annia said as she straightened up from her crouch. "That looks like a pretty good hiding spot, don't you think?"

I followed her gaze to the large oak tree standing toward the back of the yard. It shared the space with a barbecue grill and a swing set. Cradled in its branches was a treehouse. Not a very big one—the space was made for children, and I doubted more than one adult could fit up there very comfortably. A rope ladder dangled from below the house where it jutted out of the tree. As we got closer, I could see there was a trapdoor up there.

"By the Ur-god," Annia said quietly, her dark gaze on the ratty curtains rippling in the two windows that had been cut into the plywood walls. "It has to be freezing in there. How could she have survived out here for more than one night?"

"With lots of blankets, probably." The chilly breeze brought Cerlina's scent to me, laced with fear and magic. She knew we were here. "I don't think we'll both be able to fit in there, so I'll go up. You stay down here and keep a lookout."

I grabbed onto the rope ladder and gave it a firm tug. Once I was confident it could hold my weight, I climbed up easily. When I reached the top, I placed my palm against the trapdoor and gave it a light push, expecting it to open. But it didn't budge, and the wood felt a lot warmer than it should, given the weather. It was almost as if someone were sitting on it….

"Cerlina," I called. "I know you're there. Can you move out of the way so I can come up?"

Silence. Then, "You're strangers. I don't talk to strangers. Go away!"

"That's very smart of you," I said, keeping my tone light and friendly. "I bet your mother taught you that, didn't she? She's worried sick. Your father and Uncle Melan are too. They asked me to find you and bring you home."

"I c-can't come home," she said, her voice trembling through the wood. "I can't let them find me."

"You mean the Testers?"

More silence. Then, "How did you know?"

"I found the empty potion flask in your room. Can you please let me come up? I promise I'm not here to hurt you, or take you anywhere you don't want to go."

The floorboards creaked as Cerlina moved her weight off the trapdoor, and I sighed in relief. Once I was sure she was out of the way, I pushed the door open, then clambered into the small space. The ceiling was maybe five feet tall—too low for me to stand up—so I pushed the trapdoor closed, then squatted down and leaned against the back wall. Cerlina was sitting in the opposite corner only a few feet from me—the space was probably no more than seven-by-seven feet total. Her hazel eyes were round with fear and suspicion, and she clutched the blanket around her tighter. There were more blankets in the corner. On the floor, empty wrappers and boxes of junk food were scattered about, as well as a few books.

These were all expected and normal things to find with a girl hiding in a treehouse. But what I didn't expect was the warm air circulating inside the cabin. The breeze filtering in through the curtains should have been icy, but it was as warm as a sunny summer day.

"You're using your magic to keep the place warm, aren't you?" I said admiringly. "That's very intelligent of you."

Cerlina blushed, looking away. "You don't mind? I thought shifters hated magic." She glanced furtively toward me again, and I knew she was looking at my shifter eyes.

"Not all of us do. And I couldn't hate you for using your magic to survive." In fact, I was very impressed with her ability to control and use her magic at such a young age. I didn't have that kind of control, and I was eight years older.

Cerlina's expression shuttered. "Is the testing over yet? I want to go home, but I can't until after the Testers have gone."

"Cerlina, there was no test." I smiled gently, suddenly understanding. "There were rumors going about that there would be, weren't there?"

"Y-yes. I was told they were coming any day now."

"Well, there was no testing, and I don't think there will be any time soon," I assured her. "Those rumors are very unreliable, you know."

Cerlina only clutched the blanket tighter. "Yes, but they *could* come tomorrow, for all I know. And if they do, I can't be there. I can't let them take me away."

"I get it." I thought for a moment. "Do you think your parents would turn you in if they knew the truth?" Cerlina shook her head. "Then why didn't you tell them?"

"I was frightened." Cerlina sat down, curling herself into a ball. "And I didn't want Mother to worry."

"She's very worried now." Slowly, I crawled over to the little girl, then put an arm around her. "You're her only daughter, you know."

"I know." Cerlina sat stiffly for a moment, then leaned her head against my chest. "Do you think she'll be very angry with me if you take me home?"

"Maybe a little," I said, stroking the girl's hair. "But mostly, she'll be happy. And your parents will put their heads together and figure out what to do about this. We just need to get you back to them first. Now what say you and me grab some donuts to take home with you?"

***

In the end, Cerlina did come down from the tree, after writing a note to Galia to explain where she'd gone. As promised, we swung by a local bakery and picked up a dozen donuts, then took a cab ride back to the Thottings, since the three of us couldn't fit on Annia's bike together.

"I still can't believe I have her back," Mrs. Thotting

exclaimed, her arms banded tightly around Cerlina as they sat on the couch together. She kissed the top of her daughter's head. Cerlina had snuggled in close to her mother as she munched on the donut in her hand. I wondered of Mrs. Thotting realized that the girl was getting powdered sugar all over the couch, or if she just didn't care. "Thank you so much for finding her, Enforcers. I truly don't know what I would have done without you."

"Yes," the father emphatically agreed. He had Cerlina's free hand gripped tightly in his as he sat next to her on the other side of the couch. "We owe you both more than we could ever repay."

"You're very welcome, Mr. and Mrs. Thotting," Annia said, smiling. "But we were just doing our jobs."

"I will make sure to call Captain Galling personally to tell him how pleased we are that you found her so quickly," Mr. Thotting promised.

"That is an excellent idea," said Melan from where he was standing next to them. All three family members had descended on Cerlina with hugs and kisses, and more than a few tears on Mrs. Thotting's part, the moment we'd shown up on the doorstep. "And I did promise to double that bounty of yours. Let me get it for you."

"That's not—" I began, but he was already hurrying up the stairs. My stomach squirmed with both guilt and delight—was it right to take that extra money, when the Guild was already paying a bounty? But then again, servers got tips for giving good service. Maybe this was the same kind of thing?

"What are you going to tell the school?" I asked, even

though it was none of my business. "We won't mention anything about Cerlina's...abilities...in our report, but I'm sure you'll have to tell the school something."

"We'll inform them that she's gravely ill, which will give us time to sort out our affairs," the father said. "An old academy friend of mine has a successful accounting practice in Naraka. I can probably get a job there, and then we'll transfer Cerlina into one of the local schools."

"Naraka?" Cerlina asked, sounding fearful. She bit her powder-caked lip. "Daddy, that's all the way across the ocean. How will I be able to see Galia, and what about Grandma Tillie and Uncle Melan?" Tears began to fill her eyes.

Mr. Thotting's face softened, and he cupped his daughter's cheek. "We won't, not unless they come to visit. If you don't want to go through with the magic wipe, then we can't keep you here in the Federation. All the states here do magic wipes."

Cerlina began to cry in earnest, and Mrs. Thotting also looked distressed at the prospect of having to leave their friends and family behind. The parents excused themselves, and Mr. Thotting gathered Cerlina up in his arms and carried her upstairs, murmuring soothingly all the while. I swallowed against the lump in my throat as I watched them go, feeling both relieved and saddened about the family's decision.

"What an awful choice to make," Annia said quietly as we rose from the couch. "My father was a merchant marine, and he often took trips to Naraka. It's a two-week journey each way, and passage is expensive. They won't be able to come back very often, if ever, or bring family out to visit."

"It's a tough choice," I agreed. "But better than the

alternative. And at least she has loving parents who will be with her every step of the way." That was more than I'd had—my mother had been loving, but I'd never had a father. After my mother died, I'd had no one until Roanas scooped me up. He was the closest thing I'd ever have to a father...but for all that we cared for each other, he still wasn't my real parent.

We were just about to leave when Melan hurried back down the stairs. "Apologies for the wait," he said, holding a brown leather purse. He tossed it to me, and though it was not fat, it made a very satisfying *clink* in my palms as I caught it. "That should be roughly equivalent to the bounty."

"Thank you very much," I said, tying the bag to my belt. I wanted to peek inside, but I had a feeling that might be rude. "We appreciate your generosity."

"You're welcome." The man glanced between us. "Thank you so much for everything you have done. I can only hope Marlin will be able to get Cerlina safely out of the country before anyone finds out."

"If they do, they won't hear it from us," Annia promised.

"Thank you," he said with feeling. A puzzled expression crossed his face, and he added, "I do wonder where she got her talent from. She's the first to be born with magic in the family, that I know of."

"That is pretty strange," I said, knowing all too well how unwelcome and inconvenient magic could be. "Good luck to your family."

We bid Melan goodbye, then left him and his family to their uncertain, but hopefully bright, future.

***

"By Magorah, this is so bittersweet," I said over my beer. Annia and I had gone back to the Guild to fill out our report, then back out to grab a celebratory beer at a nearby bar. It was only four o'clock, but there were few hours left in the day and we'd just closed the case, so I didn't feel guilty about leaving early.

"Yeah," Annia agreed. "We solved that case in record time, and got ourselves a nice bounty, but I feel so bad about that little girl. I would have been crushed if I'd had to leave the country at her age."

I nodded. "Yeah, but she'll adjust. Once she learns the local language in Naraka, I'm sure she'll have friends in no time."

"That's true." Annia pulled out the check the Guild had issued to her and set it on the table. "So how do you want to split this? Should I just keep this, and you take the gold?"

"Yeah, I think that's the easiest." There was no way for me to cash a check anyway—I didn't own a bank account yet. Giving in to temptation, I reached beneath the table and drew out one of the coins from the pouch still tied to my belt. "I wonder how Melan was able to afford this," I mused as I held the piece of metal up to the light. The coin had a faint, not entirely pleasant smell…like some kind of weird floral extract.

Geranium oil, I realized with a jolt.

"Yeah, I'm not sure either." Annia shrugged, then narrowed her eyes as she noticed me stiffen. "What's wrong?"

"Nothing." I slipped the coin back into the pouch before Annia could inspect it further. "I was just thinking about what would have happened if there really *had* been a test at the school. The Testers would have immediately been suspicious if Cerlina had been missing."

"You're probably right." Annia pursed her lips. "In a way, I guess it was good that she chose to run now, instead of during an actual test. And that we were the ones that found her."

We finished our beers, and Annia ordered another round. As I waited for the bartender to bring us our drinks, I stared into my empty mug and struggled with my conscience. Melan was obviously involved with those bank robbers—his pretense of job hunting would be the perfect cover for scouting out additional targets. If I turned him in, then used him to track down the rest of his gang, I could snag a sizable share of that humongous bounty.

You'd be able to get a new apartment and a steambike, easy, a very tempting voice whispered in my head. *And you could buy yourself new leathers, like Annia's.*

That was true. But if I did that, I'd draw attention to Cerlina's family, and very possibly prevent them from leaving the country. No, I wouldn't have that on my conscience. Someone would catch these guys eventually, hopefully after they'd left Solantha and moved on to more lucrative prospects. Better to let sleeping dogs lie, and give that little girl a chance at freedom.

A chance you'll never really have, a bitter voice pointed out.

Maybe. But I'd solved my first case, and I had some money now. I'd have to wash the gold thoroughly. Even then, I wouldn't be able to use it safely for another couple of months. But between now and then, I'd earn more bounties and establish my reputation. I wasn't about to give up my integrity just so I could take the easy path to riches. I'd earn that steambike, and that new apartment, by protecting the innocent. That was the reason I'd signed up for this job in the first place.

A movement from the corner of my eye distracted me, and I turned to see a couple making out by the pool table. The sight of them locking lips stirred up my ever-growing hormones, sending a flush through my body. Maybe I'd head back to Witches' End and spend a bit more time with Comenius. He was cute, and there'd been a spark between us that I was very much looking forward to exploring.

"What's that grin on your face?" Annia asked as our beers came. "Your moods change like the wind, Naya."

"Nothing. Just realizing that life is pretty good, that's all. I solved my first case, and I've made a new friend." I lifted my glass to her. "That is, if you'll have me."

Annia laughed, then clinked glasses with me. "You're a wild one, Sunaya Baine, but I'll be happy to have you at my back. I have a feeling you and I are going to get into a whole lot of trouble together, and I wouldn't miss it for the world."

"Now that's something I can drink to." I said with a grin. And so, we did.

The End

Thank you so much for reading TESTED BY MAGIC! I hope you enjoyed it. If you'd like to find out more about my books, as well as new releases, exclusive excerpts, contests, giveaways and more, please *subscribe to my newsletter by visiting www.jasminewalt.com. If you enjoyed this book, I would love it if you could take the time to leave a review on Amazon. Reviews help us authors so much, and we really do appreciate each and every one. <3*

If you're new to the Baine Chronicles Series, visit www.amazon.com/dp/B016V9LOW6 to download a sample of *Burned by Magic*, where Sunaya's adventure truly begins!

Burned by Magic

The Baine Chronicles:
Book One

In the city of Solantha, mages rule absolute, with shifters considered second-class citizens and humans something in between. No one outside the mage families are allowed to have magic, and anyone born with it must agree to have it stripped from them to avoid execution.

Sunaya Baine, a shifter-mage hybrid, has managed to keep her unruly magic under wraps for the last twenty-four years. But while chasing down a shifter-hunting serial killer, she loses control of her magic in front of witnesses, drawing the attention of the dangerous and enigmatic Chief Mage.

Locked up in the Chief Mage's castle and reduced to little more than a lab rat, Sunaya resists his attempts to analyze and control her at every turn. But she soon realizes that to regain her freedom and catch the killer, she must overcome her hatred of mages and win the most powerful mage in the city to her side.

Chapter One

"Hey, shifter girl!" a human with sandy hair shouted as he leaned over the bar counter. He waved his hand as though I were a cab he was trying to flag down. "Can I get another whiskey over here?"

"Coming right up." Fighting the urge to roll my eyes, I grabbed a glass from beneath the counter and the requisite bottle of liquor. Strobe lights bounced off the dark walls of the club as I splashed a generous amount into the shot glass and slid it across the glossy countertop. The place was in full swing tonight, shifters, humans and mages all clamoring for their shot of liquid courage so they could go rub their bodies all over each other on the dance floor and hopefully take someone home with them tonight.

"Thanks." The human threw back his shot in one go. His pale cheeks turned bright red, and his wheezing cough told me taking shots was a new pastime.

"Another," he gasped, slamming his glass down on the counter.

I arched a brow. "Don't you think you should take it easy?"

The human grimaced. "I need it if I'm going to ask that girl over there for a kiss."

He jerked a thumb over his shoulder, where a brunette in a skin-tight red dress leaned against the wall, her dark orange gaze scanning the crowd. The lack of whites in her eyes combined with the dark orange color of her irises told me she was a tiger shifter, likely here searching for a male to help her get through heat.

"Why her?" I glanced back at the human, taking in his white polo shirt and short, neatly trimmed hair, which was so different from the loud clothing and hairstyles the residents of Rowanville boasted. This boy was from Maintown, the section of Solantha reserved specifically for humans, and I doubted he'd ever set foot into the melting pot of Rowanville in his life.

The boy bit his lip. "I lost a bet, and now I have to get a shifter girl to kiss me. Unless you'd rather do the honors?"

"Ugh. No thanks." The kid looked all of nineteen years old; at twenty-four I had *some* pride.

"Aww, c'mon." The kid leaned forward, desperation in his eyes. "The guys are watching me from across the room right now. If I did it right now I could get out of here."

"Save it, kid." I curled my lip, exposing the fangs sliding out behind my gum line. The kid blanched. "I'm not getting involved. My advice, you hightail it outta here and go tell your mother. That girl over in the corner is looking for a lot more than just a kiss. She'll tear you apart if you lead her on and then try to ditch her later."

"Fine." The boy slumped back down into his barstool and gave me a sullen glare. "Just give me the shot."

Why did I even bother?

"Suit yourself." I poured him another and watched him down it. He wasn't the first to come in here on a bet. Most of the human customers were regulars who knew the deal – so long as you were within these walls you treated everyone with the same amount of respect regardless if they were shifter, human or mage. That's how it was supposed to be in Rowanville – the only neighborhood in Solantha where shifters, humans and mages lived together. But every once in a while someone from one of the segregated neighborhoods wandered in to cause trouble. Usually they got more than they bargained for.

"Thanks." The kid slapped a coin down on the bar. "Wish me luck."

Yeah, right. I shook my head as he disappeared into the crowd, then turned back to my work. Tempted as I was to watch the tigress wipe the floor with him, I had a bar to tend, and it was nearly as packed as the dance floor.

I reached for the coin the kid had left for me on the counter, intending to pocket it. But as soon as I touched it, searing pain shot straight through my fingers.

"Oww!" I dropped the coin like it was a hot coal, and shook my smoking hand. Fucking Maintowner. Didn't he know shifters were allergic to silver? The little bastard had probably left it there on purpose. I had half a mind to drag him back out of the crowd so I could beat on him myself.

"I'll trade that for you." Cray, the other bartender, offered. He pocketed the coin, then handed me a pandanum coin of the same value. He was a black-skinned human, and didn't have any issue handling the silver.

"Thanks." I smiled at him and tucked the coin into one of my pouches. Most of the humans around here were pretty decent.

"Hey. Can I get a glass of *teca* with a twist of lime?" a woman with ice-blue shifter eyes asked. My nose told me she was a wolf.

"Coming right up." I ducked beneath the bar to grab the bottle of liquor. I could use a little *teca* myself – it was one of the few substances that could actually get shifters drunk. On another night, I could have been that wolf shifter, standing at the bar asking for a drink after a long day chasing bounties. Instead I was here serving them up.

As I reached for the liquor bottle, the inside of my forearm brushed against the crescent knives strapped to my leather-clad thigh. A familiar longing seared the inside of my chest, and I sighed.

All it would take is one blowjob, and you'd be out of here and back to your real job.

I fought the urge to shove my hands into my mass of curly hair and yank on it until I'd come to my senses again. There was no way I was wrapping my lips around that dick's... well, dick. I'd much rather stay here at The Twilight, even if that did mean dealing with snotty little shits like that Maintowner.

Still, being stuck behind the counter like this sucked. Yeah, I could mix a decent drink, but I wasn't meant to be a bartender. As a black panther shifter I was a natural hunter, much better suited to chasing down criminals and turning them in like every other licensed Enforcer in the city. That's what we do – we clean the riffraff off the streets so the mages don't have to get off their entitled asses and do it themselves. And since we get paid per head, most of us are pretty motivated about the whole affair.

Unfortunately for me, Garius Talcon, the Deputy Captain of the Enforcer's Guild, was in charge of distributing all the mission dockets. And ever since he found out that I was only half-shifter, he'd been treating me like a lesser being. Recently he'd decided that if I wanted to continue getting jobs I needed to get down on my knees and suck him off.

I'd told him that if I ever got down on my knees in front of him he'd better run like hell because it meant I was going to rip his balls off and feed them to him. And ever since then we'd been at an impasse.

I'd tried going to Captain Galling, but my word was useless against Talcon's, and there was no one to corroborate my story. Truthfully, it was better not to draw attention, because as far as Talcon and Galling knew I was a shifter-human hybrid. If I gave them a reason to dig deeper, they would find out about my real heritage, and money would be the *least* of my problems.

Until I figured out a way around Talcon, the only Enforcer jobs I was getting paid for were the ones I brought in by answering the emergency response calls broadcasted by my Enforcer bracelet. As much as I hated to admit it, right now bartending paid the bills.

Turning my attention back to work, I served up the *teca* with a big, fat smile on my face, and was rewarded with a big, fat coin for my trouble. I nodded my thanks at the she-wolf before she disappeared into the crowd – the shifters here were always my best tippers.

"*Sunaya!*"

I nearly jumped out of my skin at the sound of my mentor's

voice in my head, calling my name. Heart pounding, I scanned the crowded bar for him, though part of me wanted to simply shrink behind the counter and pretend I didn't exist. Even though Roanas Tillmore knew about my bartending job, I didn't like it when he saw me here – after all the time and effort he put into training me it was shameful that I was tending bar for a living. But I caught no sight of him, and weeding through the hundreds of clashing smells, I didn't catch his scent either.

Shaking my head, I picked up another glass to get started on the next order. Must've imagined it. Mindspeech didn't work well from more than a couple hundred yards away, so if I couldn't smell him then he wasn't here.

"Sunaya! Co... quick... need..."

The glass slipped from my fingers as Roanas's garbled voice echoed inside my ears. It hit the ground and shattered, tiny pieces shooting across the floor, but I hardly noticed as acid-sharp panic filled my lungs – panic I realized wasn't from me at all, but from Roanas.

As the Shiftertown Inspector, Roanas rarely ran into a situation he couldn't handle. If he was able to reach me with a mental call from afar, he was in big trouble.

"Hey!" Cray snapped as he tapped me on the shoulder. "What the hell are you doing, standing around with all this broken glass everywhere!"

I whirled on him, baring my fangs. "I have to go," I growled. He took a step backward, his eyes wide – Cray was a big guy, but as an unarmed human he was no match for me.

Turning away, I slapped my palm on the counter and launched myself over the bar. Patrons yelped as I sailed over their heads, and Cray cursed me, but I hardly heard them over the blood pounding in my ears. I landed in a crouch halfway from the bar to the door, then sprinted outside to where my steambike was parked on the curb. I was going to lose my job over this, but I didn't care – nothing mattered more to me than Roanas.

With that thought taking up all available real estate in my mind, I hopped onto my bike and shot into the street, leaving a white-hot cloud of steam in my wake.

***

Twenty minutes later, I skidded to a halt in front of Roanas's house in Shiftertown. The lights spilling out from the windows and into the darkness of the street told me he was home. I charged up the steps of the two-story brick townhouse, my veins full of fire as I prepared to face an army of enemies. I fully expected to open the door and find the place wrecked, the furniture splintered and the floor splattered with blood, because nothing short of a fucking army would be able to take down Roanas.

Instead, I found him lying on the red and gold carpet in the living room, his big body splayed next to the coffee table.

"Roanas!" I was at his side in an instant, an icy fist of fear squeezing my heart. He was lying on his back, his skin pale beneath his dark complexion as he shook. Foam spurted from his blue lips, and his tawny lion-shifter eyes rolled.

"Fuck, fuck, fuck," I chanted as I scrambled for the vial of antidote I kept in one of the pouches strapped around my torso. I knew the signs he was exhibiting all too well. This was silver poisoning.

I carefully positioned Roanas's head in my lap, then pried open his mouth and poured in some of the antidote. The pale amber liquid trickled right out of his icy lips, but I tried again, doing my best to get it into his mouth despite the tremors. Still nothing. I bit my lip as his cheek came into contact with my hand – his skin was frigid – and then tried a third time. Finally, his throat bobbed and the liquid stayed down.

Instantly the tremors receded to slight vibrations, and his breath came a little easier. A huge wave of relief rushed through me, and I wanted to sag against the couch. Instead, I fed him the rest of the antidote, drop by drop until the entire vial was gone. Even so, the symptoms did not completely subside – his lips were still blue, his skin ice-cold.

"Sunaya," Roanas croaked in a voice like crushed gravel. He shifted his head in my lap, his black mane of tiny braids sliding against my legs.

"Shhh," I soothed, sliding my arms beneath him so I could lift him onto the couch. His dark cotton shirt was soaked in sweat. "Don't speak. You need to conserve your energy."

"No… point…" he said with a weak chuckle. My leg muscles flexed as I rose to my feet with Roanas cradled in my arms. I carefully deposited him atop the couch, then sat down next to him and pulled his head into my lap again. "I'm dying."

"No," I said firmly. I ran my hand through his braids, pushing them back from his clammy forehead. "You just feel like you're dying. Which is perfectly understandable since you just experienced silver poisoning, but –"

"The antidote… wasn't enough." He wrapped his long fingers around mine, and a tremor went through me – his grip, normally so strong, was as weak as a newborn babe's. "Too much silver... too fast. Not... going to... make it."

"What the fuck is that supposed to mean?" I snarled, tightening my grip on his hand. This wasn't real. This wasn't happening. Roanas was only eighty years old – not even close to middle-aged for a shifter. He had a long, full life ahead of him, at least another two hundred years or so. Fuck, he was supposed to meet me tomorrow afternoon for a sparring match. Dying was *not* on the agenda.

"How could this happen to you?" I choked out as the tears spilled down my cheeks. "You... I... you'd never be so stupid as to accidentally poison yourself with silver!"

Shifters are hypersensitive to silver, so if it's within fifty yards of us we'll catch a whiff of it. The only reason I'd been burned by the coin earlier was because I'd been distracted. There was no way Roanas, who could hit a moving target with a chakram a hundred yards away – thirty more than my personal best – would miss such a thing.

But the empty glass lying on its side on the carpet told me that Roanas had done exactly that, and I couldn't understand why. Leaning over, I picked up the glass and sniffed it, certain I would catch the scent of silver.

But I scented absolutely nothing except the burning stench of liquor and a hint of saliva.

"What... how?" I gaped down at the glass as if it were a foreign species clutched in my palm, and to me, it might as well have been. "Why don't I smell anything?"

"The silver was mixed... with some kind of chemical... that masked the taste and scent." Roanas panted the last word, his voice edged with pain. My heart ached at the sight of his pale skin and strained expression.

JASMINE WALT

"That's why none of the others… detected it either."

"There are others?" My throat tightened. "As if it isn't bad enough you're dying." My voice broke on the last word.

"Please, Sunaya." Roanas's fingers curled around my jacket collar, pulling me closer. Even though he was sinking fast, his tawny eyes burned with a ferocious intensity. They cut through the fog of tears and pain in my brain, demanding my attention. "You must find out… who did this. There are other shifters… being targeted. Not just… about me."

"Targeted?" My eyes narrowed as my brain tried to catch up with the implications of that. "Targeted how? And why?"

"The facts… are in my case file…" Blood spilled over Roanas's lower lip, and I blinked back tears. "The Enforcers have been slow… to put the different cases together… but they are related." His voice strengthened. "I was investigating… and so they've taken me out. You must connect the dots, Sunaya. Find out who did this. Stop the killings, avenge me, and… and…"

"And what?" Shards of ice scraped along the walls of my insides, the fear inside me painfully sharp. I gripped Roanas's hand hard enough to grind the bones against each other, holding on for dear life. I never wanted to let him go.

"And… be careful."

His face went slack then, the life gone from his eyes. And as he slid from this world to the next as silently as the hot tears rolling down my cheeks, I vowed not to rest until I caught the bastard who did this.

Want more? Visit www.amazon.com/dp/B016V9LOW6
to get your copy on Amazon today!

Glossary

Annia: see under Melcott, Annia.

Baine, Sunaya: a young half-panther shifter, half-mage with a passion for justice. Because magic is forbidden to all but the mage families, Sunaya is forced to keep her erratic power a secret and faces the threat of execution if she is found out.

Baine, Mafiela: Chieftain of the Jaguar Clan and Sunaya's aunt.

Baro: capital of Inara, one of the fifty states of the Federation.

Big Leo: a gangster boss and owner of brothels in the seamy part of Maintown.

Blackhorne, Elin: a human enforcer.

Black Market: an area in Solantha where illegal items can be purchased, by night, at the buyer's risk.

Brennan, Galia: a ten-year-old schoolgirl who lives in Rowanville with her parents, Mr. and Mrs. Brennan.

Canalo: one of the fifty states making up the Northia Federation, located on the West Coast of the Northia Continent.

Canalo Council, usually just the **Council**: a governmental body composed of eight senior mages, supposed to advise the Chief Mage.

Central Continent: the largest of the continents on Recca.

Madam Charming: former owner of a shop for magic items in Witches' End.

Chief Mage: each of the fifty states of the Federation is ruled by a Chief Mage. Together, they form the Convention that meets every other year in the capital, Dara.

Comenius Genhard: a hedgewitch from Pernia, owner of the shop Over the Hedge in Witches' End.

Creator: the ultimate deity, worshipped by all three races under different names.

Crowley: human enforcer, Foreman of the Main Crew.

Downtown: the seamy area of Maintown, especially at night, when the Black Market is operating there. Full of brothels and gaming dens.

Enforcer: a bounty hunter employed by the government to seek out and capture wanted criminals. They operate under strict rules and are paid bounties for each head.

Enforcer's Guild: the administrative organization in charge of the enforcers. Also, the building from which the various enforcer crews work under their respective foremen.

Firegate Bridge: Solantha's best-known structure, a large red bridge spanning the length of Solantha Bay. It is accessible via Firegate Road.

Garai: a powerful and populous country in the east of the Central Continent, ruled by a Mage-Emperor.

Captain Galling: the human captain of the Enforcer's Guild in Solantha City, appointed by the Chief Mage.

Drombus, Melan: human, brother to Mrs. Coralia Thotting and uncle to Cerlina Thotting.

Hedgewitch: a variety of mage specialized in earth-based magic.

Inara: a state of the Northia Federation.

Larina: a runaway girl.

Kan Zao: a mental and physical martial art tradition from Garai.

Mages Guild: the governmental organization that rules the mages in Canalo, and supervises the other races. The headquarters are in Solantha Palace. They are subordinate to the Chief Mage.

Magorah: the god of the shifters, associated with the moon.

Main Crew: the largest group of Enforcers in the Guild. They are generally favored over the other crews and get the most lucrative dockets.

Maintown: the largest part of Solantha, inhabited almost exclusively by humans.

Mara: Cerlina Thotting's school friend.

Melcott, Annia: a young human enforcer.

Melcott, Noria: Annia Melcott's precocious younger sister.

Mrs. Melcott: Annia and Noria Melcott's widowed mother.

Naraka: a country off the Eastern Continent, consisting of several large islands.

Nebara: one of the fifty states making up the Northia Federation.

Noria: see under Melcott, Noria.

Northia Federation: a federation consisting of fifty states that cover the entire northern half and middle of the Western

Continent (which, in turn, is made up of Northia and Southia). Canalo is part of this federation.

Over the Hedge: a shop at Witches' End which sells magical charms and herbal remedies, belonging to Comenius Genhard.

Pernia: a country on the Central Continent.

Prison Isle: an island in the middle of Solantha Bay that serves as a prison for Canalo's worst criminals.

Ralla: a human enforcer, member of the Main Crew.

Roanas see under Tillmore, Roanas.

Rowanville: the only neighborhood of Solantha where all three races mix.

Shifter: a human who can change into animal form and back by magic; they originally resulted from illegal experiments by mages on ordinary humans.

Shiftertown: the part of Solantha where the official shifter clans live.

Shiftertown Inspector: a shifter chosen by the Shiftertown Council to police shifter-related crime.

Solantha: the capital of Canalo State, a port city on the west coast of the Northia continent, home of Sunaya Baine.

Solantha Bay: spanned by the Firegate Bridge, the bay gave its name to the city and port that became the capital of Canalo.

Solantha Palace: the seat of power in Canalo, where both the Chief Mage and the Mages Guild reside. It is located near the coast of Solantha Bay.

Testing: schoolchildren in Canalo are tested for magic at least twice during their schoolyears, and a positive result will lead to the magic wipe (often with permanent mental damage).

Thotting, Marlin and Coralia: a human couple living in Maintown.

Thotting, Cerlina: a young human schoolgirl, daughter of Marlin and Coralia Thotting.

Tillmore, Roanas: lion shifter, the Shiftertown Inspector and father figure/mentor to Sunaya, whom he rescued from the streets when she was homeless.

Ur-God: the name the humans call the Creator by.

Lord Vengar: Chief Mage of Canalo and ruler of the state.

Mrs. Weaver's School for Girls: a private school in Maintown, attended by Cerlina Thotting.

Witches' End: a pier in Solantha City, part of the Port, where immigrant magic users sell their wares and services.